Secret of the Three Treasures

Secret

of the

Three

Treasures

Janni Lee Simner

Holiday House / New York

Copyright © 2006 by Janni Lee Simner
All Rights Reserved
Printed in the United States of America
www.holidayhouse.com
First Edition
1   3   5   7   9   10   8   6   4   2

Library of Congress Cataloging-in-Publication Data
Simner, Janni Lee.
   Secret of the three treasures / by Janni Lee Simner.— 1st ed.
      p. cm.
   Summary: While pretending to be the heroine of her father's adventure novels, Tiernay
discovers new friends, buried Revolutionary War treasure, and answers to a long-ago
mystery.
   ISBN-13: 978-0-8234-1914-2 (hardcover)
   ISBN-10: 0-8234-1914-2 (hardcover)
   [1. Interpersonal relations—Fiction. 2. Buried treasure—Fiction. 3. Mothers and
daughters—Fiction. 4. Divorce—Fiction. 5. Mystery and detective stories.] I. Title.
   PZ7.S594Se 2006
   [Fic]—dc22   2005043536

For Randi Mason, for stories shared.

With thanks to Marella Sands, who was there
when Tiernay West was born; Larry Hammer,
who never stopped believing in Tiernay;
and Jennifer J. Stewart, who helped Tiernay
find a home.

Chapter 1

Tiernay West stalked through the forest, silent as the great cats of the African plains, deadly as the fabled Royal Assassins of Arakistan. With the eyes that had gotten her dubbed "Little Eagle," she scanned the verdant undergrowth, searching for the treasure hidden within.

Some motion made her pause. The shifting of a leaf, a scent upon the humid wind—with a single fluid motion she was up among the branches of an ancient oak. Adjusting her hat against the slanting sun, she settled in to watch. To wait.

"Tiernay! Tiernay, come out here this instant!"

I remained hidden among the branches of my favorite oak, not moving, not breathing. Well, trying not to breathe. You'd think that if Houdini could stay underwater for four minutes, if T. J. Redstone could conceal herself in the airless tomb of Arakistan's Hidden City for nearly a quarter hour, I could hold my breath long enough for Mom to cross the back-yard.

I tried to breathe out slowly, through my nose, the way T. J. did when hiding behind the curtains of the Arakistani ambassador's chambers, waiting for him to reveal the location of the Lost Amulet of Kazir. But instead, my breath came out in a noisy rush, through my nose and my mouth and probably even my ears. I shifted among the branches, sending autumn leaves crackling to the ground.

Mom looked sharply up. "Tiernay Markowitz, what are you doing up there?"

"Tiernay West," I said, all need for stealth gone. "My name's Tiernay West." Why is it so hard to get people to call you what you want?

Mom sighed. She enjoyed sighing, especially around me. "West is not what it says on your birth certificate."

"That's what it says on the covers of Dad's books."

"It's a pseudonym, Tiernay. That's different." Mom and I'd had this discussion before.

"You changed your name after the divorce. Why can't I change mine?"

"When you're eighteen, you can do whatever you want. Until then, you'll do as I say."

But I didn't want to wait until I was eighteen to do cool stuff. I wanted adventures now.

"Right now," Mom went on, "I say you're to get down here and put on some decent clothes. Or have you forgotten we're meeting Greg for dinner in less than an hour?"

Of course I hadn't forgotten. Why else would I be hiding?

"Tiernay . . ."

"All right, all right." I climbed down a few branches, then jumped to the ground.

My landing wasn't quite worthy of the great cats of Africa, but it was close. I only scraped one knee and ripped my pants. And my hat—broad-brimmed and woven from pale straw, a gift from Dad when he visited the Amazon to write *The River's Secret*—stayed on my head, as all true adventurers' hats do.

"Tiernay, be careful!" Mom shouted, as if I were still up in the tree, and not right there beside her. "One of these days you're going to get yourself killed."

"I'm always careful," I said, as I stalked past her across the yard and toward the house.

Just like T. J. Just like Dad.

The trouble is, Mom doesn't understand about adventuring.

She and Dad used to argue about it all the time, back when they were still married. Dad travels a lot, researching his books, and Mom complained she never knew when he was going to run off to Bangkok, or Marrakech, or Algiers.

This isn't like the old days, when adventure waited at every turn—when the world was still filled with unscaled mountains and undiscovered ancient cities. Most people don't even call themselves adventurers anymore. They're anthropologists, or journalists, or gentlemen of leisure. But there's more adventure out there than most people think, if you know where to look.

Just ask T. J. Redstone. Well, you can't ask her, because she's the heroine of Dad's books. But if you could, that's what she'd tell you. Her business cards even say PROFESSIONAL ADVENTURER on them.

But don't ask Mom. Mom's idea of an adventure is leaving Connecticut long enough to catch a Broadway play or attend a business meeting in Manhattan. Or maybe trying to get me to ballet class each week. Though I'm better about ballet now that Mom's letting me take karate, too.

Either karate or ballet would have been better than dinner with Greg.

Don't ask me about Greg, who's more interested in talking about theater and classical music than ancient cities or secret passages. Or about his son, Kevin, who hardly says anything to anyone. Or about the whole idea of Mom having boyfriends.

I climbed the stairs to my room. Books and clothes and homework papers lay scattered about. A map of the world had fallen from the wall, and one corner was caught in my underwear drawer. A half-eaten tuna sandwich and a can of root beer sat on my desk. Mom said once that looking for anything in my room was like digging for buried treasure. I'd vowed never to have a clean room again.

I flopped down on my bed. Across from me my bookshelves were half-empty. Most of the books were on the floor—books about adventurers like Lawrence of Arabia and Captain Cook and Ernest Shackleton. A couple of battered T. J. novels were on the bottom shelf, along with my map collection. The top shelf had Dad's travel books; he writes travel guides as well as T. J. stories, though they're not as interesting.

If Dad were here, we wouldn't be heading to some fancy dinner, that's for sure. We'd be exploring the streets of Manhattan with a metal detector, or hunting for ancient artifacts in the Metropolitan Museum of Art, or maybe just braving Dad's cooking, made with secret spices that taste a little like the black stuff at the bottom of the pot. But these days I only see Dad holidays and summers, which isn't nearly often enough. Mom says that's not much less often than I saw him before, given all those research trips. But adventurers like Dad and me *have* to travel—another thing Mom doesn't understand.

More T. J. books were piled on my bed. So was a pile of clothes, Mom's idea of what I should wear to dinner with Greg: A skirt. A silky blouse. Tights and shiny black dress shoes. T. J. Redstone wouldn't be caught dead in a skirt and dress shoes. She probably wouldn't be caught alive in them, either. But when Mom sets out my clothes, the dress code is nonnegotiable.

I went into the bathroom to clean my scraped knee. Then I peeled off my jeans and sweatshirt and changed, even though the tights itched and the shoes pinched my feet. Mom talks about being practical a lot, but there was nothing practical about the outfit she'd set out. The shoes even had heels, making me feel weird and wobbly as I walked.

Sir Edmund Hillary and Tenzing Norgay could

never have scaled Everest in these shoes. I doubt Dad could even have caught a plane connection at Heathrow Airport in them.

"Tiernay! They're here!"

I brushed my tangled hair into a ponytail, grabbed my hat, and stumbled downstairs. I no longer had the grace of a creature of the African plains. I didn't even have the grace of a minor house cat.

I followed Mom out to Greg's car. He always seemed to be changing cars; this one was a sort of shiny gray. Dressed in a suit the same shade of gray, complete with tie, Greg stood by the front passenger door. Sometimes I think he chooses his cars to match his clothes. Not like me; most days my socks don't even match. Mom used to complain about that, until I mounted an expedition to find out where the missing socks went. I didn't find out, but I did learn that when someone puts up a sign that says GUARD DOG ON PREMISES, they probably mean it. After that, Mom decided that mismatched socks were better than rushing me to the emergency room. I told her the bloody gash in my knee came from jumping the fence and not from the dog, but she didn't listen. And she says I suffer from an overactive imagination.

Greg opened the car door for Mom, then for me. I slid into the backseat; it was made of the sort of plush material you're always afraid to spill things on.

"Hi," Kevin mumbled, not looking up from the other side of the seat. Dirty blond bangs fell into his face. He wore a suit and tie, too, but he didn't seem to care.

"Hi," I muttered back, staring out the window as the car started up. In the window's reflection I saw him take out a video game. If Kevin wasn't going to talk to me, I wasn't going to talk to him, either.

I watched the sun set and the streetlights flicker on, wondering whether I could jump out the door and make my getaway. Probably not, in these shoes.

At least the ride was quick. A valet took our car, and I waved him off, the way I imagined T. J. would before venturing into a hotel to inquire about local guides. Mom glowered at me. Then she saw my hat, and she glowered harder. But at least she didn't say anything. She rarely did in front of Greg.

We walked inside. The restaurant was dimly lit, meaning no one would have seen how I was dressed, anyway. The waiter pulled out our chairs and set napkins in our laps.

"What a lovely place you've chosen," Mom said.

"Even if we can't see anything," I added.

Kevin shrugged. "It's only food. What's to see?"

"May I get anything to start you off?" the waiter asked.

Greg glanced at the wine list. "A bottle of your best Bordeaux for me and the lady."

"I'll have——" I began.

"A Coke," Mom said firmly. She probably still remembered the last time we'd gone out, when I tried to order Rattlesnake Venom. Mom took one look at the ingredients and said I wasn't old enough to drink it. Then she took another look and said she wasn't old enough to drink it, either. She said it probably wasn't made from real rattlesnakes, anyway.

"A Coke," I agreed. As the waiter wrote this down I added, "In a wineglass, please. With a touch of lemon. Shaken, not stirred."

Mom rolled her eyes, but the waiter smiled. "A Coke for the gentleman as well?" He nodded toward Kevin.

"No ice," Kevin said. "And no lemon. I'm allergic."

I looked at Kevin with sudden respect. "What happens if you eat lemons?" I asked in a hushed voice. If my best friend Jessie eats peanuts, she can die instantly.

Kevin shrugged, as if imminent death meant nothing to him. "I get really sick. And I barf up the lemons."

"Oh," I said, trying not to let my disappointment show. I wondered what it'd be like to go adventuring with deadly allergies. Probably it wouldn't matter, unless food got scarce. Then you might have to decide between instant death by lemons or slow death by starvation. Or you could just eat fried crickets. Dad says fried crickets are pretty tasty, especially with a good dipping sauce.

The waiter left menus with us and departed. I opened mine; it was mostly written in French. For a moment I thought it wouldn't matter what I wanted, because I couldn't read anything. In Dad's books T. J. Redstone knows seventeen languages. Dad himself knows at least six or seven. I know two, if you count Pig Latin.

But below the French descriptions, in smaller, italicized type, were English descriptions. And the moment I read them, I knew I'd found true adventurer food.

"Cool!" I said just as the waiter came back with our drinks. He'd added not only lemon, but also two cherries and a slice of lime. He set my Coke down—

in a wineglass—in front of me and nodded gravely. I nodded back.

I sipped my drink slowly, seriously.

Kevin got a wineglass, too, one with nothing but Coke in it. He stuck in his straw and started slurping. *He* never could have moved undetected through the Hidden City.

"May I take your orders?" the waiter asked.

"The prime rib for both of us," Greg said, indicating himself and Mom.

"With a side of your cheese-stuffed mushrooms," Mom added.

Kevin didn't even glance at his menu. "I'll have a hamburger. No ketchup."

"Are you allergic to ketchup, too?" I asked.

"I don't know," Kevin said. "Why take any chances?"

Adventurers live to take chances. Clearly, Kevin was no more of an adventurer than Mom.

"And for the young lady?" the waiter asked.

"I'll have the steamed mussels," I said at once. "With a side order of fried squid. And an appetizer of . . . " I scanned the menu. "Snails."

Mom choked on her drink, but Greg only chuckled. "The escargot here are excellent," he said.

After the waiter took our orders, he left. Mom and Greg started talking—about Mom's PR business, about Greg's architecture firm, about some computers that had been stolen from my school.

Kevin kept slurping his Coke. I kicked the legs of my chair, stared into my drink, and hoped the food would arrive soon.

Around me people at the other tables talked in quiet voices. Something about Wall Street and stocks at one table, about a new movie at another, about buried treasure at a third.

Buried treasure? I sat up straighter, listened closer.

"Every town has a story like this," a woman said. "Out west it would be bandits fleeing the posse with their ill-gotten gains. Here it's Revolutionary War patriots on the run, forced to bury their gold in some cave when the English got too close. Never mind that Connecticut's not exactly riddled with caves. The legend says the gold's still out there, waiting to be discovered by some sufficiently percipient soul."

"That's me!" I said. Greg raised a curious eyebrow in my direction.

"Just a legend," a deep-voiced man said, as if legends were scarcely worth bothering with.

A lesser adventurer might have let that deter her. But I knew better. The best adventures always begin with legends that no one believes.

I set down my glass, got to my feet, and strode straight to the table where the couple sat.

"I'm your man . . . umm, woman," I said.

The man looked up from his wineglass. "Excuse me?"

"If there's lost treasure to be found, I'm the one to find it." I bowed deeply, sweeping my hat out in front of me. "Tiernay West, Professional Adventurer—at your service."

Chapter 2

Tiernay West stared at her clients across the restaurant table. Or rather, her potential clients, for they hadn't yet agreed to her terms.

The choice of venue had been hers, of course. She only frequented the best restaurants. Good adventurers didn't come cheaply, after all, and few were as good as West. She'd find their gold—for a price. She met the couple's eyes with her own unflinching stare. She could afford to wait.

She knew what their answer would be.

"Tiernay, what do you think you're doing?" Mom grabbed my shoulder. "I'm so sorry—" she began, speaking to the man and woman at the table.

I pulled free of her grip, put my hat back on my head, and spoke to the couple. "You said you were looking for buried treasure." Not the most eloquent introduction, but I didn't have time now for anything else. "I can find it for you. That's my job. I'm an

14

adventurer, see." Technically I was an adventurer-in-training, since I hadn't completed any adventures yet, but that was about to change. I hoped.

The man shook his head, seeming annoyed, but the woman smiled. "Well, you wouldn't be the first to search for Revolutionary War gold." She ran a hand through her graying hair. "Or even the least qualified."

"Then I've got the job?" I fought to keep my voice calm, professional. Adventurers never squeak when they're excited. They never cross their fingers, either, at least not where anyone can see.

"You're as welcome as anyone to try," the woman said.

No promises, then. But she was willing to wait and see what I could do. I could deal with that. I lifted my head. "You won't regret this, I promise." I tapped the edge of my hat. "Is there anything you feel I should know before I get started? Any place you'd recommend I might look?"

I felt Mom's hand on my shoulder again. I tried to pull away, but this time she didn't let go.

"You might try the library," the woman said, still smiling. "That's where I always begin."

"The library. Right. I'm on it." And then Mom did drag me away, not loosening her grip until we were back at our own table.

"I've never been so embarrassed in my life," Mom said, but I knew that wasn't true. She'd been at least as embarrassed when I'd knocked over Mrs. Lamb's teacup last spring, checking for poison. She said Mrs. Lamb was an important client. I said that made it all the more important to see to her safety.

An adventurer does what an adventurer has to do.

And right now what I had to do was find that gold. This could be my big break. Just like stumbling onto the Fabled Ruins of Estavapol had been for T. J. in Dad's first novel, *Adventure's Path*. (Dad's big break hadn't come until two books later, when *Whispers of the Past* became a best seller.)

"When we get home—" Mom was saying.

Greg laid a hand on her arm. "Let it go, Sylvia."

"Yeah," Kevin said. "The food's here."

The waiter set plates down in front of us. White china, decorated with flowers and edged with gold trim. Adventurer food really ought to be served on dented tin dishes in the jungle, but no one had asked me. Lifting an elegant silver fork—it was decorated with flowers, too—I started on my squid.

Adventurer food, I quickly discovered, was very rubbery. Almost as rubbery as Dad's cooking.

I chewed. And chewed. And chewed some more.

"The food here is excellent," Mom said.

"Yeah," Kevin muttered. "It's okay." He was halfway through his hamburger and on his third Coke. He wouldn't have stood a chance against a professional poisoner. Not unless it was someone who only worked with ketchup and lemon slices.

I kept chewing. Unlike the squid, the snails were more squishy than rubbery.

"Excuse me, miss?"

I looked up, my mouth full of buttery snail. The lady with the buried treasure looked down at me. "Good luck on your adventure," she said. Behind her, her companion snickered. Let him laugh; he clearly wasn't my client.

"Thank you," I told the woman. Only it came out as "Thmf yoo." I swallowed hard. Half-chewed snail went down in a slithery lump.

Mom looked like she wished a hidden mine shaft would swallow us both. "I'm sorry my daughter disturbed you—"

The woman waved a dismissive hand. "No trouble at all, Mrs. West. I admire her enthusiasm."

"Keane," Mom said.

"Pardon?"

"I'm Sylvia Keane."

"And I'm Jane Grey." The woman smiled and held out a hand. Mom shook it. "There've been Keanes in this town a long time, haven't there? Keanes and Jensens, all the way back."

"I suppose so," Mom said, as if it wasn't very important.

Jane Grey turned back to me. "If you find anything on your adventure, I'd love to know. I specialize in these sorts of stories." She took a business card out of a silver case and handed it to me. JANE GREY, FOLKLORIST, the card read. NORTH CENTRAL UNIVERSITY. I grinned. Folklorist was another one of those words, like journalist or anthropologist.

"It's an honor to meet a fellow adventurer," I said.

"The honor's mine." She smiled once more, then departed.

I turned back to the table. "See," I told Mom. "She didn't mind. True professionals never do."

Mom just let out a long sigh and buried her face in her hands.

"How long have there been Keanes here, anyway?" I asked. I knew Mom had lived here all her life, except when she went to college in New York. Grandma and Grampa Keane had lived here, too, until they retired to Arizona three years ago.

"Oh, I don't know," Mom said. "Since at least the Revolutionary War, I suppose."

"So that might be our gold hidden in that cave!"

Mom took a sip of her wine. "I doubt that, Tiernay."

But adventurers know better. We look at all the possibilities. I went back to my chewing, formulating a plan of action as I did.

You'd think libraries would carry books on the things that really matter.

A catalog search on Buried Treasure turned up two books on oil drilling, three books on mining, a catalog of tulip bulbs, a novel titled *Love's Windswept Embrace*, and a guide to investing in real estate.

Buried Gold gave me books on autumn leaves, raising children, the Connecticut wine industry, and caring for fine china.

I did no better with Lost Gold, Missing Gold, or Gold in Caves. I left the computer catalog and tried browsing the local history section instead. To my surprise the first thing I found was a thin volume on

The Keanes of South Newbury. I flipped through the pages. The book looked like it had been typed by hand, then photocopied.

The role of the Keanes in the Revolutionary War is but a footnote to historians today, but even at the beginning of the twentieth century, their name was well-known. . . .

Mom was wrong. Her family—my family—*was* important!

Tiernay Keane, Professional Adventurer. No, it didn't work.

I kept reading anyway, wondering what sort of cool people—cool heroes, no doubt—Mom and I were descended from.

The book stopped talking about the Revolutionary War, though, and started talking about weddings and babies and family trees. I put it aside for later, and turned to the guidebooks instead. I found seven books on Connecticut—three of them claiming to be comprehensive—but none of their indexes had any listings under Gold or Treasure, buried or otherwise.

I threw the last guidebook to the floor, then sighed and bent to retrieve it. I'd only been here a couple of hours, after all. In *Whispers of the Past,* T. J. Redstone spent six months in the Lost Library of Alexandria, and I bet she didn't stop when a catalog search failed to turn up anything under Assassins. For that matter, Dad used to spend weeks at the library before starting each new book. He forgot to come home for dinner sometimes, which drove Mom crazy. Actually, it bugged me a little, too.

"Planning a vacation?"

I looked up to see the librarian looking down at me. I slid the guidebook back onto its shelf. "I'm looking for treasure," I told her.

The librarian nodded. "Plenty of that in a library. What sort of treasure did you have in mind?"

"Buried. Or maybe hidden. In a cave, during the Revolutionary War."

"Oh, well, we have plenty of books on the Revolutionary War."

And on dishes, and children, and tulip bulbs. "But none on buried treasure?"

"If you mean the X-marks-the-spot, start-digging-here sort of treasure, I'm afraid not."

I knew better than to expect my task to be that easy. Besides, the one time T. J. found a treasure map, the only thing the X marked was an ambush.

"Gold and silver were in pretty short supply during the war, anyway," the librarian said. "The colonies used coins from other countries when they could, or else printed their own paper money."

"But it's gold I'm looking for." Jane Grey had been quite clear about that.

"Well, you could try a web search. Only I'm afraid we close at two on Sundays. And it's almost two now."

I sighed once more, then stopped myself. Sighing wasn't a very adventurerlike thing to do. I lifted my chin, adjusted my hat.

"Thank you for your assistance," I said as politely as I could.

"You're quite welcome. Would you like to check anything out?"

I followed the librarian to the counter and handed her *The Keanes of South Newbury*. As I did, a slip of folded, yellowed paper fell out from between the pages.

I stared at the paper reverently, wondering if I'd discovered an ancient manuscript.

I unfolded it carefully. It had a raggedy edge, as if someone had pulled it out of a spiral notebook. Spiral notebooks weren't ancient at all. Neither was the purple ink in which someone had written:

Three treasures they took from us during the War.
The first we found again.

The second was lost, yet may be recovered.

But the third is gone—gone beyond recall.

Yes! I clutched the paper in my hands. Sometimes even not-so-ancient manuscripts hold valuable information.

Three treasures, I thought. I wondered if I could find them all. Just a legend, indeed. I wondered whether those treasures had belonged to my ancestors, the famous Keanes of South Newbury, whose name had once been well-known. I vowed I'd do everything I could to reclaim the treasures.

I folded the paper carefully and slipped it back into the book the librarian handed me. I glanced at the library's computers, eager to find out more. But then I glanced at the clock above those computers, and I knew the library could help me no more today.

It was time for more desperate measures.

Bent over the handlebars of my bicycle, I raced through the streets of South Newbury, past rows of houses, up and down familiar hills. Small hills. As Jane Grey, Folklorist, had said, Connecticut didn't have lots of caves and mountains.

But it did have treasure. Three treasures—except

one of those treasures had already been found. And another, the third, was lost beyond recall.

The Healing Springs of Juaraja were lost beyond recall, too, yet T. J. Redstone found them, anyway. Good thing, or she would have died of deadly snakebite, and Dad wouldn't have been able to finish *The River's Secret*.

I'd find the third treasure, and the second one, too.

My straw hat hung down my back as I rode, along with my backpack. I wore a plastic bicycle helmet painted brown and green. An adventurer's hat has to change to suit her purposes.

My bicycle was painted the same colors as my helmet. It had originally been bright pink, but I'd quickly fixed that. A pink bicycle could never be hidden in a forest or camouflaged in a jungle while I fled from my enemies. I'd taken off the bright orange flag that came with the bicycle, too. Mom had drawn the line, though, when I wanted to remove the reflectors. "You don't need to be that stealthy," she'd insisted.

The knobby tires weren't stealthy, either, but they did get me where I needed to go. I looked left and right, then crossed a bright green lawn, threading my way between a flamingo and a lawn gnome. The bicycle bounced as I rode through a rock garden, but I kept my seat.

This was an ATB, after all. An all-terrain bicycle.

"Oh, look, it's jungle girl!"

I turned to see Brooke Sanders sitting in her front yard. Or on a chair in her yard; even back in kindergarten, Brooke would never sit on the floor. She hated getting her clothes dirty.

Brooke and I had been friends for a while in kindergarten, but then one day I led her through a huge puddle so we could climb a tree and spy on the second graders. We both wound up covered in mud, but while my mom just sighed a lot, Brooke's mom grounded her for a week. Brooke wouldn't have anything to do with me after that.

She sat in her chair, stringing tiny beads onto a bracelet. "What are you planning to do?" she asked. "Go on a safari?"

"Maybe." I came to a stop as I answered. Dad had gone on a safari once. He'd wanted to take me along, but Mom wouldn't let him. She said she didn't want me catching some strange disease, like malaria or yellow fever. Also, she said I couldn't miss that much school.

Brooke reached for another bead. "I'm starting a club," she said.

"What kind of club?" I didn't want to join or anything, but adventurers are naturally curious.

"It's a secret." Brooke shrugged. "Not that it matters to you. You're not invited."

"Well, you're not invited on my safari, either!" I started pedaling again.

Behind me I heard Brooke laughing. I pedaled harder.

I coasted down a hill and bounced across a trickling stream. Here the stream was surrounded by green grass and picnic tables, but outside of town it joined the deeper Newbury River, bubbling through forests and alongside steep bluffs.

I pumped up another hill and pulled into a driveway. A long driveway, with a shiny gray car parked in front of the garage. I left my bicycle beside the car and changed back into my regular hat. Squaring my shoulders, I climbed the steps to the front door and knocked.

No one answered. I knocked again, then rang the doorbell for good measure.

"All right, all right." Footsteps trudged inside the house, and the door swung open. Kevin stood there, in a T-shirt, jeans, and bare feet, looking annoyed. "What do you want?"

"I need," I said in my coolest adventurer voice, "to borrow your Internet connection."

For a long moment Kevin stared at me, and I was sure he would refuse. I'd asked Mom to get us an account of our own, but she said her office connection was sufficient to meet her needs and the computers at school were sufficient to meet mine. Except now most of the school computers had been stolen.

I was about to ask Kevin again when he shrugged. "Yeah, sure. Whatever." He gestured me inside and led me through the house.

I'd been here before, with Mom, for dinner a few times. Unlike Dad, Greg really could cook. But (also unlike Dad) he'd never even tried to broil shark fillets or alligator tails.

As we passed his office Kevin's dad called out, "Is that a friend you have over, Kevin?" He sounded surprised, as if Kevin didn't have friends over often.

"No," I called back. "This is just a business visit."

Greg glanced up from his desk. "Oh, hi Tiernay." He smiled, then returned to the blueprint spread out in front of him.

I followed Kevin upstairs to his room. The table with his computer stood against one wall; it took up more space than his bed did. CDs and papers were scattered all over the table, but the rest of his room was pretty neat—bed made, floor clean. I wondered whether Kevin was allergic to dirty laundry, too—or maybe just afraid to take a chance on finding out.

He gestured to the desk chair. "Make it quick. I just got *GraveBuster IV* this morning, and I haven't had a chance to try it out yet."

I pulled up Kevin's web browser and clicked Search. Mom's computer at work and the computers at school all make a lot of noise when you run them, but Kevin's machine was perfectly silent.

Under Search Terms I entered "Buried Treasure."

874,000 results, the computer replied.

"Add some modifiers," Kevin mumbled, looking over my shoulder.

I typed "Buried Treasure"+"Keanes."

No matches.

Kevin shuffled from one foot to the other. He picked up a CD from his desk and looked at the case. "The animation for this game is supposed to be awesome." He sounded almost excited for once. And impatient.

"Hang on," I said. I tried "Buried Treasure"+ "Jensens." Jane Grey had mentioned Jensens, too, after all.

"What do you want with the Jensens?" Kevin asked.

"You know them?"

"Sure," Kevin said. "So do you. Katie's in our class, remember?"

"Oh." Katie Jensen didn't seem very adventure-some. I'd assumed Jane Grey meant some other Jensen. I turned back to the screen.

1 match found, the computer said. And below that, a link read: **Welcome to Buried Treasure Antiques**.

"Yes!" I clicked on the link. The page loaded quickly.

Under construction, it said. **Please come back soon**.

"Oh, that's just Katie's dad's shop," Kevin said.

"What?" I stood and whirled around, knocking the chair over behind me. Kevin knew a place that not only specialized in buried treasure, but whose owners had been in South Newbury since before the Revolutionary War, just like mine? Why hadn't he told me?

Kevin moved to pick the chair up, but I grabbed him by the shoulders. "Tell me," I said, hoping the intensity of my gaze would convey how important this was. "Tell me everything you know."

Chapter 3

Tiernay West walked the streets of the Old City, exotic colors and mysterious scents swirling around her. She paused before a fishmonger's stall, examined the smelly carcasses piled there, and moved on. She stopped next beside a stall piled high with woven straw baskets. She picked one up, but even as she did, someone took it from her hands, giving her another instead. West nodded, though she didn't dare open the basket's lid, not here.

She knew the information she sought was within.

"It's just an old antique shop," Kevin said. He pulled away from me and opened his CD-ROM drive.

"How would you know?"

"I've been there." He gave a bored shrug, put the CD in place, and closed the drive. "Mr. Jensen's place has old computers sometimes. I fix them up and donate them and stuff."

"Computers aren't treasure," I said.

"Not to you, maybe."

I stared at Kevin's computer screen, which went black as the game loaded. As T. J. said when she was searching for the Whistling Sword of the Keroon, there's always more to a situation than meets the eye. If you know how to look at it.

The Jensens had been around as long as the Keanes. Maybe our ancestors were steadfast friends during the war. Maybe the Jensens knew about the three treasures, too.

Besides, you don't name a place Buried Treasure Antiques if you don't have some experience with treasure. That would be false advertising. I pulled a notebook out of my backpack. "Do you know where this buried treasure place is?"

"Umm, sure. Here." Kevin scribbled down an address. "But they're only open till five on Sundays."

That meant I'd better hurry. I shoved the notebook into my backpack and started for the door.

"Don't bother thanking me or anything," Kevin said.

"Thanks," I said as I stepped through the doorway. Behind me Kevin's computer made a groaning noise, the first sound I'd heard from it all day.

"Begin the adventure of a lifetime!" a voice boomed from the machine. I glanced back, startled, but all I saw was Kevin holding a game controller, and some sort of picture on the screen. I continued down the stairs and out to my bicycle.

I had a *real* adventure to pursue, after all.

When T. J. Redstone got lost in the South Pacific, she held a hand up to the wind. Based on its direction and her knowledge of the prevailing autumn winds, she found her way back to shore.

As far as I could tell, South Newbury had no prevailing winds in October. The dry leaves on the ground blew first one way, then another. When I wet a finger and held it to the air, I just wound up with a cold finger.

I'd found Knowlton Lane, where the buried treasure shop was supposed to be, but the street ended before I got to the number I needed. I'd ridden around and around, past stores that sold food and clothes and all sorts of other things, but not past any place that sold buried treasure.

"You'll never find it if you keep going that way."

I skidded to a stop. Kevin rode up beside me.

"What are you doing here?"

"*GraveBuster* was lame. I couldn't get the graphics to work right or anything." Kevin tightened his grip on his handlebars—padded handlebars. His bicycle was black, with silver stripes and thin racing tires that would never make it across a harsh savanna or through a steamy jungle. Something that looked like an antenna was attached to the frame. The reflectors were the same green as Mom's old alarm clock, and they kept pulsing on and off.

"Who are you trying to be?" I asked. "James Bond?"

"Who are you trying to be? Indiana Jones?"

I didn't answer that.

"Anyway," Kevin said, "the antique shop is down this weird little side street. You'll never find it if you keep riding in circles."

"I wasn't riding in circles. I was following the prevailing winds."

"Whatever. You want me to show you where it is?"

I almost told Kevin I didn't need his help. But then I thought of how Roald Amundsen could never have reached the South Pole without his loyal companions. Well, those companions included his sled dogs, some of whom were turned into dinner on the way back to civilization, so maybe that wasn't the best example. But T. J. never could have made her way past the Chattering Stones in *Songs of Death* without the help of the One-Eyed Seer, either, and he was rewarded handsomely in the end.

Sometimes an adventurer doesn't get to choose her native guides.

"Lead on," I told Kevin, hoping that he wouldn't expect to be handsomely rewarded. I'd tried explaining to Mom that adventurers have expenses, but she still wouldn't raise my allowance.

We left the street and followed a dusty alley, bounding fearlessly over rocks and debris. Well, I bounded fearlessly over them, anyway. Kevin worked his way carefully around each obstacle. My all-terrain bicycle took every bump, every curve without damage. Kevin's bicycle didn't bump at all, not even when he hit dips in the pavement, maybe because of the shock absorbers around his front wheel.

We turned onto a narrow street more smoothly paved than the alley and coasted past a cluster of shops. Hale's Imports. Putnam's Map and Atlas Center.

Buried Treasure Antiques.

I was off that bicycle in a flash. Kevin began looking for a place to lock our bikes. I left him to his work and strode into the shop.

"Cool!" I said the moment I stepped inside.

Stuff was everywhere in this place. On tables, on shelves, crammed into corners. All sorts of stuff—silver platters, old Lego pieces, crystal wineglasses, plastic Barbie dolls (okay, Barbie's not cool; she has weird feet and her clothes fall apart—not good qualities in an adventurer), dusty books, elegant wooden chairs that didn't match, old vinyl records. . . .

The treasures I sought could easily be hidden here, or else information that would lead me to those treasures. I dug right in and began searching.

I picked things up off shelves and examined them carefully. I might find a treasure map, or a secret compartment, or even another old sheet of notebook paper. Maybe there were some letters from the Keanes to the Jensens, or the Jensens to the Keanes. I could leave no stone unturned.

"Excuse me, miss, but these toys aren't for children."

I looked up, one hand clutching a rusty old jack-in-the-box (there'd been no letters or maps inside), the other about to reach for a pale green wineglass. A man in jeans and a rumpled shirt stared down at me through tired eyes.

"I'm not looking for toys." I stretched to my full

four feet seven inches and tapped the rim of my hat. Or tried to tap it, until I realized I was still wearing my bicycle helmet. "I'm looking for clues. Perhaps you can help." I held out a hand. "The name's West. Tiernay West, Professional—"

"That's nice." He took the jack-in-the-box from my hands. "Now go play outside, all right?" He returned to the front of the shop. A woman stood near the cash register, dressed in heels, skirt, and jacket, like Mom on workdays. She held a clipboard in one hand.

"I'm not playing," I said, but the man didn't hear. After a moment I went back to my searching.

A bell in the doorway chimed as Kevin stepped in. "Hi, Mr. Jensen."

The man—Mr. Jensen—glanced up. He didn't look like the descendant of Revolutionary War heroes. "Sorry, Kevin, we don't have any computers today." He turned back to the woman.

"The insurance company will need a description of the stolen items for our files," she said.

Stolen items? I set down the jewelry box I'd been examining—there was nothing hidden beneath the ugly velvet lining—and listened.

Kevin walked up beside me. "You find what you're looking for?"

"Shhh." I leaned forward, straining to hear. Kevin wandered off and began flipping through a rack of comic books.

"There was only one item," Mr. Jensen said wearily. "An old sword dating back more than two centuries. It's a family heirloom, one of our only possessions to survive the Revolutionary War."

Heirloom was another word for "treasure." I listened harder. An ancient sword certainly qualified as treasure.

The woman pursed her lips together and made some notes on her pad. Mr. Jensen went on, "The police already have all the details. I came in and found the door open and the sword missing from its place above the hearth." He pointed to a wooden mantel. Below the mantel stood a dusty oil painting of flames in a fireplace, propped up inside one of those baskets you put logs in. Above the mantel was nothing at all, just some empty hooks. Which I guess was his point.

The woman frowned. "Your insurance policy is contingent upon having a fully functional alarm system in place."

"It is fully functional! Or was." Mr. Jensen ran a hand through hair as rumpled as his shirt. "I already told the police; I don't know why it malfunctioned. No one has the code but me and my wife. I have no interest in the insurance money, if that's what you're thinking."

The insurance woman raised a skeptical brow, as if that was exactly what she was thinking.

"My ancestors fought with that sword," Mr. Jensen said. His voice grew hard and a little angry. "Timothy Jensen said powder could get wet and muskets could misfire, but you always knew whether your sword had an edge. He carried the sword with him into Massachusetts and the Battle of Bunker Hill; he lost it while retreating with Washington's troops across New Jersey. It took my family decades to recover the sword after that. I have no desire to be the one who loses it again, I assure you."

"I see," the insurance woman said, as if she didn't.

I saw, though. I drew a sharp breath. *Three treasures they took from us during the War. The first we found again.*

The sword was the first treasure; it had to be. Lost and then found. Except now Mr. Jensen had lost it again.

Only—what was the treasure doing with his family in the first place? The piece of paper I'd found had been in a book on the Keanes, not the Jensens.

Shouldn't that sword have been used by my ancestors? Shouldn't it have hung over our fireplace?

The insurance woman wrote more notes. "I'll go ahead and file this claim," she said. "Assuming the police investigation turns up nothing more, and the item fails to be found—"

"But it has to be found!" I blurted out. No matter whose family it belonged to.

Mr. Jensen and the insurance woman both turned to stare at me.

"I'll find it." I strode boldly forward. "Allow me to introduce myself—"

My foot caught on the edge of a floor lamp. The lamp teetered forward, and I reached out with both hands to catch it.

And apparently with both feet, too. My legs slid out from under me, and I crashed to the ground, taking a box of Lincoln Logs, a silver serving platter, and an entire jar of tiny glass beads crashing down with me.

Not to mention the lamp.

I grabbed the lamp in time, twisting heroically and making sure it fell on top of me, rather than under. It didn't break.

Fortunately, Lincoln Logs and silver platters are

sturdier than lamps. They didn't break, either, though they did make lots of noise as they clattered to the floor. The beads skittered off in every direction, but they were too small to break.

In other words, a successful recovery—danger averted, no damage done.

Not that Mr. Jensen saw it that way. As soon as I put the lamp down, he grabbed my arm and hauled me to my feet.

"What do you think you're doing?" he demanded.

"Trying to help us both." I looked straight into his eyes. They were still tired-looking, at odds with his angry voice. "Trying to find your lost treasure."

"What right do you have to come barging into my shop?"

The sign on the door said OPEN; what other permission did I need? Clearly this was a trick question. I didn't answer.

"I told you," Mr. Jensen said, his voice rising, "that this shop is not for children. Now go outside, and get into trouble elsewhere. Please." He let go of me and pointed sharply toward the door.

I almost left right then. Obviously Mr. Jensen didn't appreciate the services an adventurer could provide.

But as I started toward the door I saw a small, almost imperceptible smile cross his face. Maybe he was just glad I was leaving.

Or maybe he had something to hide. I whirled back to face him. It was my turn to ask questions.

"When," I asked in my most professional adventurer voice, "did you first discover the sword was missing?"

"Out," he said.

"When did you first realize it might be of—of outside interest?"

"Now!"

I tried a different approach. "How did the sword first fall into your hands?"

"I mean it!"

I stood my ground, waiting for answers. After a moment Mr. Jensen threw his hands up. "That's it. I'm calling your parents. What's your name?"

"Tiernay West." I had nothing to hide.

Behind me someone cleared his throat. I glanced back to see Kevin kneeling on the floor, picking up glass beads.

"West?" he mouthed.

I shrugged. Since school still called me Tiernay

Markowitz, he'd probably never heard my real name. Not that it was any of his business, anyway.

Mr. Jensen stepped behind the cash register and grabbed a phone book. "Parents' names?"

"Sylvia and Jake."

He flipped through the pages.

I turned to the insurance woman. Perhaps she would be more helpful. "When did you—"

The woman set her clipboard down. "The police report is all a matter of public record, you know. When Mr. Jensen arrived this morning, he found the lock on the door broken and the sword missing. The alarm never went off."

Mr. Jensen slammed the phone book shut. "There's no Jake West here."

I rolled my eyes. "Of course not. Dad and I don't live together."

"No Sylvia West, either."

"Mom and I don't have the same last name. Her name is Keane." I looked at him meaningfully, but if the name meant anything to him, he kept the fact well-hidden.

"Listen, young lady." Mr. Jensen's neck had turned bright red, and the red was spreading to his face. "Either you tell me how to reach your parents, or I'm calling the police."

I'm not a lawyer (few adventurers are), but as far as I could tell, I hadn't done anything illegal. I looked at Mr. Jensen. Whether he called the police or not, he obviously wasn't going to be any help. He wasn't going to answer my questions.

Not yet. But one day—one day I would deliver that sword into his hands, assuming he was the rightful owner in the first place. One day he would regret every question he'd refused to answer. But for now I could do nothing more here. I left the shop without another word.

Kevin trailed out behind me. I heard him drop the jar of beads onto the counter as he did.

I started toward our bicycles.

"What are you trying to do?" Kevin asked. He sounded worried. "Get yourself arrested?"

"I'm searching for lost treasure." Didn't anyone understand that?

"By knocking things off shelves and asking rude questions?"

"My questions weren't rude. His were."

Kevin knelt down and began unlocking our bikes. He pressed some buttons on his U-shaped lock, waited for a series of beeps, and pressed some more. Down the alleyway, the bell of Buried Treasure Antiques chimed. The insurance woman stepped out, a briefcase in one hand, and started walking away.

"Thank you for your assistance," I called after her. She didn't turn around, just walked faster, heels clattering on the uneven pavement.

"You're weird," Kevin said.

"I am not." Not compared with shop owners who put OPEN signs on their doors and then get angry when you walk in. Or with insurance people who can't even say "you're welcome" when you thank them for their help. "I am not weird. Everyone else is."

"Right, Tiernay. Or should I call you West?"

I couldn't tell whether he was joking or not. "West will do."

Kevin pushed my bicycle toward me, but I waved it away. "Not yet." I got down on hands and knees and crawled slowly back toward Mr. Jensen's shop.

"Really weird, West."

I ignored him, scouring the ground for tracks as I moved—for any sign at all of which way the sword thief had gone.

People don't leave as many tracks on concrete as they do on ancient leaf-littered forest floors. The only tracks I saw were occasional treads from a couple of bicycles—one with thin racing tires, one with knobby all-terrain treads.

I wondered how adventurers found other people's tracks before they made tracks of their own.

I inched forward, examining the ground more closely. I saw gum wrappers and bottle caps, but nothing that looked like anyone else's tracks.

Not until I crawled straight into a pair of sneakered feet.

Chapter 4

Every land possesses its own venomous creatures.

Tiernay West had faced the poisonous scorpions of the Sahara, had outwitted the man-eating Gila monsters of the American Southwest. She'd disarmed deadly rattlesnakes with both hands tied behind her back, and she'd sidestepped the poisonous ooze of seething slugs.

Let nature throw its dangers at her. Tiernay West was ready for them.

I looked up.

The sneakers were attached to a pair of long, jean-covered legs. The legs were attached to a lanky body and squinty face.

The face of Daryll the slug.

He looked like a slug, with his T-shirt and jeans and sneakers all faded to gray. Maybe he wasn't covered with oozing slime, but the sneer that turned up one corner of his mouth still made me want to step back and wash my hands—even though normally I think slime is cool and getting dirty just part of an adventurer's job.

Daryll leaned against the wall of the antique shop, looking down at me. I met his scornful gaze, reminding myself that an adventurer doesn't know fear. Not even when faced with a rival who once stole her lunch money, or flushed her book report on *The Worst Journey in the World* down the toilet, or fed her very first hat to the paper cutter in the art room. That all happened before I became an adventurer, of course. It also happened before Daryll moved on to middle school and decided he couldn't bother with anyone from elementary school anymore.

"What are you looking at, short stuff?"

"Nothing." No way was I telling Daryll there was missing treasure around.

"Liar," Daryll said. His eyes squinted even closer together. I rolled out of the way just before he kicked the spot where I'd been—an old trick of his that I knew far too well.

"Kids," Daryll said with a snort, and walked away.

I scrambled to my feet. Daryll sauntered down the street, kicking bits of gravel out of his way.

Then, in front of the antique shop, he stopped—and stepped inside.

What would Daryll want in Buried Treasure Antiques? I doubted he planned to buy some Barbies or add to his Lego collection.

"He knows something," I said.

Behind me Kevin laughed nervously. "Daryll? Daryll doesn't have enough brain cells to know anything."

"Why's he inside Mr. Jensen's shop, then?" What good is a guide if he doesn't know valuable information when he sees it?

"Maybe because his father owns the store?" Kevin said.

"Oh. Right." I knew Daryll was Katie's brother, though she never talked about him.

"It still looks suspicious," I said.

Kevin glanced uneasily toward the shop. "That's only because Daryll always looks suspicious. You ready to go yet?"

"Almost." Crouching low, I continued in the direction I'd been headed when I met the slug. When I reached Buried Treasure Antiques, I stood just high enough to peer in the window.

Daryll sat behind the cash register, looking bored, while Mr. Jensen stacked lime green bowls onto a shelf.

There was nothing more to be learned here, not today. I followed Kevin back to our bicycles.

We rode in silence to the mouth of the alley, where I brought my bike to a squealing stop. Kevin's bicycle made no noise as he pulled up beside me.

"Umm, thanks for your help," I said. "See you later."

Kevin shifted uncomfortably. "Actually, I'm supposed to follow you home."

"Why?" I didn't need a native guide to find my own house.

"Your mom invited Dad and me over for supper."

"But they just saw each other yesterday!"

"I know." Kevin nodded glumly. "And you guys don't have a computer or anything. There's nothing to do but sit around and talk."

"Parents," I sighed.

"Yeah," Kevin agreed.

Together we started for home.

As we rode, I did some thinking. If I was going to find that sword, I needed more information than anyone at Buried Treasure Antiques was willing to give me. I needed to talk to someone else. Someone who might know what was going on.

Someone who knew both Daryll and Mr. Jensen.

"I can't talk to you," Katie Jensen said.

It was Monday morning, and we were both in the school yard, waiting for the bell to ring.

"What do you mean you can't talk to me? You're talking to me now."

"I mean I'm not *supposed* to talk to you." Katie pressed her lips firmly together, and her gray eyes darted nervously about. By the monkey bars a knot of girls laughed; Brooke Sanders stood in the center of the knot. A couple more girls played jump rope by the swing set. I'd tried to join them once, but they'd kicked me out when I'd told them ropes were better for climbing than jumping. Most of the boys tossed a basketball around. Kevin stood alone against the school building playing with his game—or was it a handheld computer? Kevin was mostly alone at school. I wondered whether he considered talking to other people another risk best avoided—but some-how, I didn't think so.

I adjusted my hat—the straw one, not the bike helmet—and stared at Katie, waiting, just like T. J.

Redstone waited when the curator of the Lost Library of Alexandria said she wasn't authorized to enter the stacks. Though in the end, waiting wasn't enough; T. J. had to bribe him with some rare Arakistani coins, too.

Fortunately, Katie lacked the curator's steely will. "Brooke started this club," she whispered. "We're not allowed to talk to anyone who's not in it." Katie tugged on one of her ragged brown braids. When she was younger, she used to chew on them, and they'd never really recovered.

"Why would you want to be in a club like that?"

Katie looked at me as if it were a stupid question. "Because everyone else is." Without another word she ran toward the monkey bars. "Hey, Brooke!" she called as she ran.

Christopher Columbus could never have found America if he'd done what everybody else was doing. And T. J. Redstone would still be living in the small midwestern town she'd grown up in.

"Tiernay!"

I looked around to see Jessie Harrison walking toward me, waving. I waved back. I'd mostly been alone at school, too, until Jessie moved to South Newbury last year, after her parents got divorced.

Jessie's long skirt swept the pavement. A wool shawl, woven in shimmery colors by her grandmother, hung over her shoulders. Her reddish hair fell loosely down her back. Adventurers aren't the only ones who don't care what other people think. Kids make fun of Jessie all the time for the way she dresses, but Jessie keeps doing what she wants. Just like me.

Mom and Dad had been in the middle of their own divorce when Jessie moved here. They didn't yell like Jessie's parents, but they did have a lot of quiet talks with their bedroom door closed. Only those talks weren't as quiet as they thought, at least not once I put a glass up to the door. That's when I first learned how to gather information, a valuable skill for any adventurer. Jessie helped me figure out what the information meant. Even then, she was good at predicting the future.

Jessie reached around into her backpack—it was woven in the same colors as her shawl—and pulled out a deck of cards. "I learned a new card trick," she said. "Want to see?"

"Sure! But can you tell my fortune first?" Adventurers have their fortunes told all the time, in dim tents and the back rooms of dusty old shops.

"Of course," Jessie said. She'd learned about using cards to predict the future from her older sister. Her sister used it mostly to tell people whom they were going to marry, but Jessie's fortunes were more interesting—and more useful.

"Let's go over to the picnic tables," Jessie said. Her skirt swirled as she walked.

I followed, glancing at my watch—a birthday gift from Dad—as I did. The programmable display said it was 7:55 P.M. in Singapore, 4:25 P.M. in Kabul, and 5:40 P.M. in Kathmandu. That meant I still had a few minutes before school started.

"Cut the deck," Jessie said as we both sat down. Her voice grew deeper; she swept an arm through the air. "Madame Jessica shall tell your fortune."

I'd asked Jessie once if she'd ever thought about becoming a professional fortune-teller. If she did, we could work together for years to come. She'd said fortune-telling was just for fun, though; she wanted to be an astrophysicist when she grew up.

Maybe I'd need the services of a professional astrophysicist someday, too. Adventuring is an unpredictable business.

I cut the deck. Jessie laid cards out on the picnic

table. Lots of picture cards, and lots of diamonds and hearts.

"Ah," Jessie said in her deep, fortune-teller voice, "red is the color of love." I grimaced, but she quickly added, "And also the color of blood."

Much better.

"The cards show me a lot of—" Jessie hesitated. "A lot of excitement in your future. Unexpected challenges. What is lost will be found."

"Great!" That was just what I needed to hear.

"What is found will be lost."

"Not so great." Though maybe that had already happened, given the sword.

"Unlikely partnerships. Help from an unexpected quarter. Look to those closest to you for aid."

"I work alone," I muttered. I glanced at Brooke and Katie and the others, but they were all whispering now. "Is there anything else?"

"No," Jessie said solemnly. She glanced at the cards again. "Well, except that in fourteen years you'll marry someone who's favorite color is blue, and you'll have"—Jessie squinted—"forty-seven children."

"Ick! Jessie—"

"That is all. Madame Jessica has spoken." Jessie swept the cards away and put them into her backpack.

Across the school yard, someone screamed.

Chapter 5

Tiernay West was trained in forty-seven different fighting techniques. She'd begun with the ancient Korean art of Tae Kwon Do, but quickly progressed to ancienter arts from Mongolia, from India, from deepest Arakistan. Her reflexes were lightning fast, her every move focused and precise. Those who knew her tried not to get in her way.

Of those who crossed her, very few lived to tell the tale.

"Give that back! Give it back!"

I looked across the school yard. One of the older kids who'd been playing basketball was now tossing Kevin's handheld computer back and forth. Kevin grabbed for it, but the taller boy spun away. Kevin leaped forward again, just as the boy whirled back toward him. Kevin's head slammed into the kid's chest. The kid staggered back, and then his face turned red.

"Hey, watch it!" He threw the computer to the ground and stepped toward Kevin. Kevin turned and ran. The kid ran after him.

I may not be able to reward my guides handsomely. But I can at least help them out of trouble once in a while.

I leaped forward, into the fray. Behind me Jessie called, "Tiernay, do you really think you should—" but I didn't stop to listen.

In the karate class I'm taking, there are hundreds, maybe even thousands, of ways to disable your opponent. Unfortunately, I'd only been to one class so far, and all we'd had time for were warm-ups and going over the rules. I hadn't even gotten to kick anything yet.

So instead, I relied on the skills I already had. I let Kevin run past me, and then as the older kid followed, I stretched out my foot and tripped him.

He fell forward, toward the blacktop, blocking his fall with his hands. Out of the corner of my eye, I saw Kevin dash back to grab his computer.

"*What* is going on here?"

I looked up to see Mr. Abrams, one of the schoolyard monitors, standing over us. The older boy—I suddenly remembered his name was Seth—sat up then. His hands were scraped and bleeding where they'd hit the asphalt, and the knees of his jeans were torn, too.

An adventurer is gracious, even to defeated enemies. I reached into my pocket and handed him a tissue. He threw it back at me and wiped his hands on his T-shirt instead. Which only made his shirt bloody as well.

"What's going on?" Mr. Abrams asked again just as the bell rang. Kids headed into school, until no one was left outside but Mr. Abrams, Seth, me, and Kevin. Kevin stood a short ways off, looking nervous and not saying anything.

Seth stood up. I thought he'd try to get us in trouble, even though he was the one who'd started this, but instead, he just said, "Nothing, I'm fine," and started toward the doors.

"You're not fine, and you are going to the nurse's office," Mr. Abrams told him. "I'll check in a couple minutes to make sure you're there."

Seth disappeared into the school. "I guess I'd better get to class," I said.

"Not so fast. You and your friend"—Mr. Abrams

gestured toward Kevin—"have an appointment with the principal."

"What'd you have to mess with things for?" Kevin asked as we walked down the hall to the principal's office.

"I rescued you!" I turned to look at Kevin, but he wouldn't meet my eyes.

"Lucky me," Kevin muttered, as if getting rescued was just one more thing to worry about.

"Would you rather I'd let you wind up facedown on the pavement?"

"It's no big deal." Kevin stared at the floor as he walked.

"It is a big deal! If I hadn't—hadn't interceded when I did, who knows what Seth would have done? Mrs. Johnston will understand." At least, I hoped she would.

"Mrs. Johnston isn't the problem," Kevin said.

"Then what is the problem?"

Kevin didn't answer. He didn't say anything when we reached the principal's office, either. That left me to do all the talking. I don't mind talking, but still, Kevin could have helped out.

Mrs. Johnston was a lot better at listening than

Mr. Abrams. "Your impulse to help your friend was admirable," she said when I was through. "But next time, Tiernay, please call an adult instead of taking matters into your own hands. All right?"

There hadn't been time to call an adult, but I didn't say so. I didn't answer at all, and Mrs. Johnston decided that meant I agreed. "Now both of you had better get back to class," she said, handing me a hall pass.

Kevin wouldn't speak as we walked to class; he just stared at his feet as he shuffled along.

"Don't bother thanking me," I said.

He didn't.

I stepped into the classroom, head held high, proud of a job well done, no matter what Kevin said—or didn't say.

From the corner of the room, someone giggled. Then someone else. I glanced around and saw Brooke and a couple of other kids with their heads bent together, laughing.

"Quiet!" said our teacher, Ms. Friedman. Brooke and her friends stopped laughing, but I heard one of the boys say, "Saved by a girl, Kevin?" When I looked over, I saw Kevin's face turning red. He sank down into his seat. Someone else laughed.

What's wrong with being saved by a girl? A successful rescue was a successful rescue. People were so strange sometimes.

School was so strange. I couldn't wait until I grew up and could adventure full-time instead.

We were in the middle of math. Fractions, which aren't so bad—at least, not if you ask yourself, fractions of what? Two-thirds the distance from here to the Blue Mosque of Istanbul? That would put you somewhere near Lisbon. Three-quarters of your taxi fare from the airport to the Caracas Hilton in Venezuela? Are you trying to bargain, or do you really want to be dropped off almost four miles away?

While I worked, I thought. Rescuing Kevin had taken my mind from the problem at hand—getting Katie to talk about the stolen sword. I tore a page out of my notebook and wrote:

Katie, if you can't talk to me, can you write instead?
—Tiernay

I folded the paper up, wrote Katie's name on it, and nudged Jessie, who sat in front of me. "Pass it on," I whispered. That was the code for transporting secret messages—at school, at least.

Jessie passed the note forward, then turned back to me. "I think what you did was great. No matter what other people think."

We switched from math to spelling. I'm not nearly as good at spelling, at least not the words we learn at school. Now, words like *longitude* or *circumnavigation*—those I can spell, because I know I'll have a use for them one day.

"Pass it on," Jessie whispered, handing a couple of folded pages back to me. I saw my name on the top sheet, and I opened it. As I did, the page beneath it unfolded, too. Only then did I realize that the bottom page was addressed to Brooke, not me.

The top page said:

Tiernay, I don't know if I'm allowed to write notes. I'll check with Brooke.—Katie

An adventurer would never take orders like that.

The second note was longer—a series of messages between Brooke and Katie.

Katie, remember our meeting today. The clubhouse is in my backyard. Be there at four o'clock. If you're late, we won't let you in. —Brooke

Yes! I'd intercepted a secret missive from Brooke's club. Just like T. J. Redstone intercepting the coded communications of the Arakistani assassins in *Whispers of the Past*. Of course, it had taken her another six months to break the code. I was lucky—Brooke and Katie wrote their missives in English.

Brooke, I won't be late. I really want to join you guys. —Katie

The more I looked at it, the more Katie's handwriting seemed familiar. Probably because Ms. Friedman made us read each others' papers sometimes.

Katie, don't forget to bring something valuable with you. If you don't, we won't let you in. —Brooke

Brooke, I already have something. Something I'm sure no one else has. —Katie

Katie, what is it? —Brooke

Brooke, it's a surprise. I can't tell you until the meeting. But once I do, you can keep it at the clubhouse as long as you want. I know it'll be safe there. —Katie

"That's it!" I said aloud.

Ms. Friedman stopped writing words on the blackboard and looked at me. I turned quickly back to my notebook, folding up Katie's note as I did.

Katie had some sense, not revealing all she knew, but I saw through her words clearly enough. Stealing the sword would have been easy for her. She probably watched her dad type in the security code all the time. And Brooke's club would provide all the motivation she needed. Yet I couldn't accuse her without proof.

It was time for some covert action. Time to infiltrate Brooke's Secret Organization.

By the end of the day, I had a plan. I would go straight to Brooke's house after school, sneak into her clubhouse, and be well concealed by the time the meeting began. I'd confirm that Katie had the sword, and then I'd confront her and reclaim it for its rightful owner.

Mom had other ideas. She met me in the school parking lot, ballet bag in hand.

"I just had a lesson!" I protested.

Mom sighed. "It's Monday, Tiernay. You have ballet on Mondays, karate on Wednesdays."

"But I can't go to ballet! I have to—" I almost explained about Brooke's Secret Organization, but there were still other kids in the parking lot. Some of them might be members. "I have things to do!"

Mom gave me one of her I-don't-have-time-for-this looks. I wondered how she could possibly be related to Revolutionary War heroes. She was still in work clothes, and her briefcase lay on the seat beside her. She usually worked in the coffee shop next door during my lessons. I tried to picture George Washington planning to cross the Delaware over a caramel latte. It didn't work. Real adventurers make their plans over cups of strong, dark coffee. Or mugs of strong, dark root beer, with extra foam.

"Either you come to ballet," Mom said, "or you can skip all your lessons. On Mondays and Wednesdays both."

"Not karate!" I couldn't quit before I even learned how to kick.

Mom opened the car door. I got in.

Ballet class started with lots of stretching. That was okay; we stretch in karate, too. Then we worked on different positions—first position, second position, third position. I decided fourth position, where you're already sort of stretched out, would be the perfect position from which to heroically leap across the room.

That wasn't okay. I spent the rest of the class sitting against the wall, watching. Which was okay again, since the class was practicing pirouetting to "The Good Ship Lollipop." T. J. Redstone would never have subjected herself to such a thing.

I pulled out *The Keanes of South Newbury* and read some more as I watched. I found more names, including something about a wedding between Abigail and Thomas Keane in the 1740s. The book said, *Their son James would become infamous for his actions during the War for Independence.*

Infamous? The book meant famous, didn't it? I read faster, needing to know more, but then Mom came to pick me up.

Miss Nadine told her about my heroic leap—only it didn't sound so heroic when she described it. By the time we got back into the car, Mom was sighing again.

"Can't you just do what you're told for once, like everyone else?"

Why would Mom want me to be like Katie or Brooke? I sighed, too, and glanced at my watch— 5:45 A.M. in Melbourne, 3:45 A.M. in Beijing. That meant Brooke's meeting was already in progress.

"Can I go for a bike ride?" I asked.

Mom glanced at her watch—which only told South Newbury time—as she pulled into our driveway. "All right. But I want you home in time for dinner."

"No problem."

I went out to the shed, got on my bicycle, and pedaled hard for Brooke's house. A brisk autumn wind blew; light gray clouds moved against the sky. Autumn leaves crunched beneath my tires.

I stopped a block from Brooke's house, by a drugstore with a bicycle rack. Stealth was as important as speed, and I knew I could approach more quietly on foot.

My bike chain wasn't as fancy as Kevin's, but my combination lock did the job well enough. I looped the chain through my bicycle helmet as well, and switched to my adventurer hat.

Once on foot, I realized I was still wearing my ballet slippers. I wished I had my sneakers, but then I saw how quiet the slippers were against the pavement. *Stealth*, I thought again. *Like the great cats of Africa.*

I approached Brooke's house from the far side of the street. The driveway was empty, which meant Brooke's parents must still be at work. The front lawn was bright green and perfectly mowed; a low white fence circled a small garden. A bird chirped from the branches of a maple tree, but otherwise, the house was silent. It didn't look like the sort of place one would find a secret organization.

Which made it the perfect place, of course.

Crouching close to the grass, I crept around Brooke's house. Her backyard was neat and green, too, not filled with weeds like our yard.

I stopped to scan the terrain. And in the center of the yard, beneath a tall oak tree, I caught my first glimpse of the Secret Organization's Secret Headquarters.

Well, the Headquarters wasn't all that secret, not with the bright green and yellow boards that made up the small wooden structure. Flowers were painted on the boards, and rainbows. An attempt to make the Secret Organization seem harmless? I wasn't fooled that easily.

Even from across the yard, I heard voices inside, talking and laughing. Good. The noise would cover my approach.

I inched slowly toward the tree, setting one foot down before lifting the other. My breathing was slow, steady.

A sudden sound and I froze, willing myself to turn as invisible as a grain of sand against the shimmering Sahara. A bird flew from the grass in front of me, squawked, and disappeared into the clouds. I continued on, keeping the tree between me and the Secret Headquarters as I drew near. The tree's lowest branches formed a canopy just above the building's roof, shading its only window.

Perfect.

I tied my hat strap firmly in place. Then I grasped the rough trunk, and I shinned up. My ballet shoes caught on the bark, but I pried them free and kept climbing. I found a thick branch and inched out along it until I was above the wooden roof.

The branch began to creak. I jumped down, hitting the roof with a delicate thud.

"What was that?" someone called from inside.

"Probably just some dumb squirrel," Brooke said.

Squirrel? I was nothing like a squirrel. I was like one of the great cats. Couldn't Brooke tell the difference?

I crawled to the roof's edge, crouching just above the window. There was no glass, just a hole in the wood.

"So anyway," Brooke said, "we have a club name, and we have a secret password."

And I'd missed them, all because of ballet.

"Now on to the entrance requirements."

I leaned forward, listening. I might learn something useful today after all.

"You were all supposed to bring something valuable with you. Something no one else has; something that reflects your true nature and proves that you're worthy to be in this club. You'll have to leave it here to prove you're a member, of course. I've already qualified, by supplying this clubhouse. No one else has offered to donate a clubhouse like this, have they? That shows how generous I am."

I was sure Dad and I could have built one—we were planning to before the divorce, only his book deadlines kept getting in the way—but the other girls mumbled in agreement.

"So," Brooke said, her voice suddenly eager, "what did you all bring?"

"I brought my grandmother's porcelain music box," a girl said. I recognized her as Jillian Knowles, from my class. Around her the others oohed and aahed. "You wind it up, and the ballerina dances to the music." Strains of tinny ballet music wafted through the window. "I brought it because I want to be a dancer one day, too—"

Another girl—Francesca Rodgers—broke in. "I brought my unicorn collection." There were more oohs and aahs.

"I brought a necklace. . . ."

"I brought this crystal globe. It snows when you shake it. . . . "

Maybe this stuff was cool to some people, but it seemed no more like treasure to me than the Barbies and Legos in Buried Treasure Antiques.

"Well I brought this." At last, I heard Katie's voice.

No oohs and aahs this time. Just silence, and more silence. "Wow," Francesca finally said, but not as if she meant it.

I heard a soft hiss, like metal against leather. "Hey, careful!" Brooke yelled.

I clutched the edge of the roof and bent down, swinging my head toward the window. My ponytail flopped out of my hat. I ignored it and looked in.

In the center of the room, Katie Jensen stood, wielding a silver sword.

Chapter 6

The hilt of the ancient sword was set with emeralds and rubies, sapphires and diamonds. The deadly steel blade, tempered in forges long abandoned, shone in the slanting afternoon sun.

Tiernay West need only reach forward, and the shining artifact would be hers.

But West was an experienced adventurer. She knew better than to consider any artifact hers until she held it in her hands.

Katie did steal the sword! I now had all the evidence I needed.

"Where did you get that . . . thing?" Brooke demanded, in the same tone I might have used if Mom handed me a frilly skirt. She and Katie stood facing each other. Five other girls from school sat in a semicircle around them, facing the door.

"Your true nature is a sword?" Jillian squeaked.

"Pretty cool, huh? And you can keep it here as long as you want." Katie grinned and swung the sword through the air, stumbling slightly beneath its weight. Brooke ducked out of the way; the look on her face said she thought the sword was anything but cool.

Let Brooke think what she wanted. The steel blade was notched and tarnished, but that only meant it had been well used, used in the Revolutionary War. I couldn't think of many things cooler than that. My fingers tingled, eager to hold that sword for myself. It was so close; I could almost reach out and touch it.

Clutching the hilt with both hands, Katie slashed at the air once more, twirling around as she did.

Her eyes went wide as she turned to face the open window. She twisted her head sideways, as if trying to get a better look at me while I hung upside down. "Tiernay! What are you doing here?"

Brooke whirled at Katie's words. "Hey! She is not invited!" Hands on hips, Brooke started toward the window.

I almost leaped in and claimed the sword right then. But there were seven girls there—and one of them was armed.

An adventurer knows when the odds are against her. I scrambled back onto the roof, vowing I'd be back. Conditions weren't right for Robert Peary to reach the North Pole his first try, either.

From the roof I leaped to the ground. I landed gracefully, knees slightly bent, just like we'd practiced in ballet. Maybe dance had some use after all.

Brooke and her friends burst through the door just as I hit the ground. My feet pounded against the damp grass as I raced across the backyard and around the side of the house.

The members of Brooke's Secret Organization pursued me to the edge of the backyard; then Brooke stopped abruptly. "Oh, give it up," Brooke said. "She isn't worth it."

That meant Brooke couldn't have caught me if she tried.

I stopped and glanced over my shoulder in time to see Brooke walking back toward the Headquarters. The other girls followed her.

All but Katie. She stood still, glaring at me. At least, I thought she was glaring at me, and I glared right back, but then I realized she was looking past me. I followed her gaze and saw Daryll leaning lazily against Brooke's house. A slow, sluglike grin crossed his face.

"So that's where it is," Daryll said.

Katie just kept glaring.

"You'll save us both a lot of trouble if you hand it over now," he said.

"No," Katie said. "It's bad enough you take everything else. You can't have this. I'll hide it again. I'll hide it as often as I have to."

"I'll tell," Daryll said. His laugh reminded me of the ruthless pirates who threw T. J. Redstone overboard off the coast of Antarctica, in *Treasure Beneath the Waves.*

"I'll tell," Katie retorted sharply. "I have more to tell than you."

For a moment Daryll's expression darkened. He took a step toward Katie. She took a step away. So did I. But as soon as I noticed, I took that step right back again.

Daryll sneered. "It's not like you can stop me. I'll get it if I want it. I always do." He turned and slunk off across Brooke's lawn.

"Slug," Katie muttered. She wiped her hand fiercely across her face.

It must be tough, living with a slug. Going to school with him had been bad enough.

"What are *you* looking at?" Katie demanded, as

if noticing me for the first time. She turned and stalked back to the Headquarters. For a moment I stared after her; then I walked back to my bicycle. The sun had sunk low, and the sky was cloudier than before. I unlocked my bike and pedaled toward home.

I didn't know why Daryll wanted the sword, but I had no doubt he'd return to try and take it for himself. The only question was when. I couldn't take any chances; I couldn't assume he would wait. I needed to return before him.

Tonight, I thought as I rode. *Tonight, under cover of darkness, I'll be back.*

"*What,*" Mom demanded as I stepped in the door, "have you done to your ballet shoes?"

I glanced down. The pink slippers were torn from climbing and bicycling, and grass-stained from crossing Brooke's yard.

"You know, ballet's not so bad," I said.

As Mom stared at me in stunned silence I started up the stairs. "Are you feeling okay?" she finally called after me.

"Never better." I'd found the sword; soon I would claim it. One treasure down, two to go.

"Why does that worry me?" Mom muttered from below.

I didn't answer.

Dinner was just Mom and me, for once.

Mom made macaroni and cheese. She threw in an extra packet of cheese sauce, just for me. I helped out and made a salad with Feta cheese and olives, just for her. One thing Mom and I agree on is that most foods taste better when covered with cheese. Not like Dad, who prefers spicy sauces with names even he can't pronounce. I also eat those sauces—I *am* an adventurer, after all—but I like Mom food, too.

I stirred pepper into my mac and cheese; pepper makes any food more adventurous. "I like when it's just the two of us," I said. I'd have liked it even better if Dad were with us, but that wasn't an option. He was somewhere in Asia right now, researching the next T. J. book. "We can't eat with Greg all the time."

A troubled look crossed Mom's face, but she didn't say anything. Not until we began clearing the dishes away. "Even if Greg and I got more serious, there'd still be time for just the two of us. You know that, Tiernay, don't you?"

The mac and cheese in my stomach felt suddenly cold and lumpy. "What do you mean, more serious?" I didn't look at Mom as I rinsed my plate and put it in the dishwasher.

"I mean it's not impossible that one day you'll be seeing a lot more of Greg than you do now."

"You mean even more meals together?"

Mom didn't answer, and I knew that wasn't what she meant. She'd only said *if*, not *when*, but an adventurer considers all the possibilities. It was bad enough Dad had moved out—if Greg moved in with us, I'd be outnumbered by nonadventurers two to one. *Three* to one if Greg brought Kevin with him— which seemed likely, since Kevin's mom and stepdad live in Baltimore, and I doubt someone scared of ketchup would risk riding a train. (T. J. Redstone *always* gets attacked by bandits when she rides trains. The trains I take to visit Dad in Manhattan are mostly bandit-free, but I keep hoping.)

I reminded myself that I was Tiernay West, adventurer. If Mom and Greg "got more serious," I'd figure out something to do about it. I put the leftover salad in the fridge, then went up to my room, determined not to think about Mom and Greg for the rest of the night.

Instead, I thought about Kevin. That wasn't an improvement. Kevin hadn't spoken to me—or anyone else—for the rest of the school day. As far as I was concerned, he could rescue himself next time. If he was more scared of being laughed at than of being smashed into the pavement, that was his problem, not mine.

Yet he had led me to Buried Treasure Antiques, and he'd been there when I first learned about the sword. If I knew a sword had been stolen, I'd want to know when it was found again, even if I was no longer part of the adventure.

I sighed and went back downstairs. Mom sat in the living room going through the mail. I ignored her and went into the kitchen. For once, the cordless phone sat on its stand recharging; often it was buried beneath piles of papers, and we only found it when it rang.

Mom had Greg's number on speed dial. I hoped he wouldn't answer, but he did.

"Is Kevin there?" I asked.

"I'll check. Who is this?"

"Tiernay."

"Oh, hello." Greg's voice sounded suddenly

friendly—too friendly. Was he thinking about Mom and him spending more time together, too? Adventurers need to bribe the proper authorities sometimes. I wondered how big a bribe it would take to convince Greg to move to Jakarta.

"I'll get Kevin," Greg said. He set the phone down. I heard him and Kevin talking in the background. I couldn't make out the words, but Greg didn't sound quite as friendly as before.

"Kevin's busy right now," Greg said when he returned. "He says you should e-mail him instead."

"I don't have e-mail." Kevin knew that.

Greg hesitated a moment. "Well, why don't I take a message, then?"

I wasn't sure I wanted Greg—or anyone else—to know about the sword until I'd successfully recovered it. I wasn't even sure I wanted Kevin to know, but it seemed the right thing to do. "Just tell him that—that what was lost has been found." Or one of the things that had been lost, anyway. "It's at Brooke's house, and I'm going to get it as soon as I can. And—and that's all, okay?"

I heard a pen scribbling on paper. "All right, I'll tell him. Oh, and Tiernay?"

"Yeah?"

"I heard about what you did for Kevin today. I want you to know that I appreciate your sticking up for him."

"Umm, thanks. Thanks a lot." I looked at the phone. Who would have thought Greg, of all people, would appreciate a good rescue?

He hung up without saying anything more.

For my expedition that night, I dressed in full adventurer gear. Stealthy full adventurer gear.

Sturdy black sneakers. Dark jeans. A khaki vest with lots of pockets. A different hat—this one made of black canvas—that Dad had brought me from Europe. A pocketknife—another gift from Dad— hung from my belt. So did a flashlight, borrowed from the emergency supplies in the garage.

I couldn't go out at first dark like I wanted, because Brooke's family would still be awake—not to mention Mom. So I sat up in bed with my flashlight, reading *The Keanes of South Newbury* instead. The book finally finished with the weddings and births and got to real history. I read eagerly, hoping to learn about my family's heroic exploits at last.

Eagerly, that is, until I found out what my family's role in the Revolutionary War had really been.

The Keanes were Tories, English loyalists who didn't believe the American colonies ought to be independent. And James Keane—*infamous* James Keane—was the biggest sympathizer of them all. In 1776 when Timothy Jensen bravely fought beside George Washington on Long Island, in Manhattan, and across New Jersey, James's three older brothers were also there—fighting for the British under General Howe. James Keane preferred to stay closer to home, though, where he could try to undermine the Revolution by plotting to steal the Jensen family fortune.

Unlike the Keanes, the Jensens were well-known patriots, and they were using their money to support the war. When Timothy's sister, Emma Jensen (the book called her little Emma, even though she was as old as I was), learned what James Keane was up to, she waited for a moonless night, then snuck off and hid her family's gold. The gold was never found, and Emma was never again seen alive. In a way James Keane succeeded, because the money could no longer be used for the war.

But that wasn't the worst part. The worst part was what James Keane did find: Emma Jensen's lifeless body, floating in the Newbury River. Or rather, he said he found her; most people assumed the truth was that he'd drowned Emma himself. No one could prove that, though, so James Keane was spared the hanging he deserved. He went on to have children, and grandchildren, and great-grandchildren—all the way down to Mom and me.

I stared at the book, unable to believe it. My ancestors were traitors, murderous traitors. Katie Jensen and Daryll the slug were the ones related to heroes.

A familiar paper fell out of the book, the same yellowed paper I'd read in the library. I unfolded it again. This time, I recognized the handwriting, though it was younger and messier than I was used to. It was in Katie's handwriting, saying,

Three treasures they took from us during the War.
The first we found again.
The second was lost, yet may be recovered.
But the third is gone—gone beyond recall.

The treasures didn't belong to my family; they belonged to hers. The Keanes were the ones who took those treasures away: the gold by trying to steal it, the sword by fighting against Timothy Jensen. We'd probably taken the third treasure, too, in some awful way I didn't know about yet.

Thieves, murderers, treacherous villains—that's what my ancestors were. How could I even think about being an adventurer, with a history like that?

I moved to the window, watching the lights go off in the houses up and down my block. Light rain fell. Raindrops glistened beneath the streetlamps.

I glanced at my watch. It was lunchtime in Seoul. Surely the entire town of South Newbury now slept— including the members of Brooke's Secret Organization. If I wanted that sword, the time to get it was now.

Was I, a descendant of James Keane, still worthy to search for treasure?

I'd *make* myself worthy. I'd rescue that sword, and I'd return it to its rightful owner, Mr. Jensen. I'd find the gold Emma Jensen had hidden, too. I'd redeem my troubled past every way I could.

With a new sense of purpose, I started down the stairs. I was halfway across the living room when I heard someone behind me.

"Tiernay, where do you think you're going?"

Mom was in her nightgown, and she held a paperback—some sort of mystery with a cat on the cover—in one hand.

"To get a glass of milk?"

Mom eyed me suspiciously. "I thought you didn't like milk."

"That . . . that was last week." I hated interrogations.

"Do you always require a pocketknife to visit the refrigerator?" She looked me over. "And a flashlight?"

"Well, umm, what if the refrigerator light goes out?"

Mom sighed. "Get your milk, Tiernay. And then go to bed. And I don't want to see you wandering around in the middle of the night again. Understood?"

I was doing this to redeem Mom's past, too. Somehow I had to make her understand. "It's like this—" I began.

Mom cut me off. "Just promise me you won't go out at night without permission, all right?"

"But—"

"Tiernay, can't you just do what I say for once? Without—" she continued as I tried to break in, "arguing?"

I didn't answer.

"Tiernay." Mom's voice held the same edge it had when I'd tried to convince her that we couldn't meet Greg for a movie, because there'd been monsoons in New Delhi and who knew where they'd strike next.

"All right." I sighed. How was I supposed to complete this adventure—any adventure—if I couldn't go out at night without permission? T. J. Redstone never had these problems. Then again, T. J. didn't start adventuring until after she'd graduated college and moved away from home, much to the dismay of her parents, who'd been hoping she'd go on to medical school. As far as I could tell, leaving home wasn't an option for me, not when I hadn't even graduated elementary school.

I went to the kitchen and got my milk. After a sip I decided I still didn't like the stuff. I didn't say anything, though, just finished the glass in several noisy gulps and started back toward the stairs. Mom still stood there, waiting for me.

As I passed the living room table, I saw the cordless phone lying on top of a pile of newspapers. I had a sudden idea.

Maybe there was more than one way to obtain

parental permission. I tucked the phone into my vest and went back up to my room. Then I closed my door, and I dialed the phone.

I had another parent, after all. Whether Mom and Dad "saw a lot more" of each other or not.

The phone rang once, twice, three times. Just when I thought no one would answer, the ringing cut off.

"Jake West, here." The voice was deep, professional—and very sleepy.

"Hi, Dad!"

"Tiernay!" Dad's voice warmed up at once. He stifled a yawn. "How are you?"

"I'm fine. How are you? Where are you?" Dad had a number that forwarded to wherever he was. He only gave it to his publisher and to contacts for his books—and to me.

"Vladivostok," Dad said. "In Russia, you know."

"I know." Dad was the one who'd bought me my first atlas. "Near China and Korea, right?"

"Right." Even over the phone, I could see Dad's smile. He yawned again. I checked my watch; it was 2:38 P.M. in Vladivostok. "I'll send you a map."

"Postmarked," I reminded him. Dad sent me a map from every city he visited.

"Of course."

"So is T. J. going to Vladivostok?"

"She'd better be. Spent the past three weeks riding"—another yawn—"the Trans-Siberian Railroad for this book. Sorry, Tiernay. I just got in, so I'm not quite awake. How about I call you back a little later?"

"Sure, Dad." He really did sound tired, just like when he stayed up all night finishing a book. "Only— is it okay if I go out for a walk meanwhile?"

"I guess so, Tiernay." He sounded a little confused. "Assuming"—yawn—"that your homework is done. Listen, pumpkin, I'll talk to you later, okay?"

"Okay, Dad." The phone line went silent; I wasn't sure whether Dad had hung up or fallen asleep. After a moment I heard a click on the other end, leaving me listening to a dial tone from Vladivostok.

I almost would have put off my adventure, to talk to Dad a little longer. Well, maybe he'd be more awake by the time I returned; we'd have lots to talk about then. I left the phone on my bed, opened my door, and peered down the hall. Mom's light was off, but she might still be up. Dad had given me permission to go out, but I wasn't sure Mom couldn't take that permission away again.

I decided not to find out. I closed the door again

and walked over to the window. Silently—as silently as T. J. when she approached the Chattering Stones—I pulled the rope ladder out from beneath my bed, latched it to the window, and lowered it.

Mom often reminded me that the rope ladder was only intended for emergencies, like a house fire. But losing the sword and leaving the past unredeemed would be emergencies, too.

I turned out my light, climbed over the windowsill, and slowly made my way to the ground. The rope ladder creaked, but no one heard. The lights in my house, in all the houses on my block, remained off. Rain still fell, very lightly; the air held a cool, wet-dirt smell. Streetlamps lit my way as I crossed my yard and started down the street. I would have taken my bicycle, but I wasn't sure the rack in back would hold a sword.

Back at my house, I heard the phone ringing. I walked faster, just in case Mom woke up and noticed me missing.

At Brooke's house, like everywhere else, the lights were out. I started across her yard. In the dark I could just make out the shadowy bulk of Brooke's Secret Headquarters.

Something rustled in the trees behind me. I froze,

waiting for the sound to move on. Instead, the rustling stopped. Someone was behind me, watching me. Daryll?

T. J. Redstone says there's nothing worse than having an enemy at your back. I whirled around and shone the flashlight right in the rustler's face.

"Hey, turn that thing off, West." The voice was familiar—but not at all sluglike.

"Kevin, what are you doing here?" I turned the flashlight off.

Kevin shrugged. "Dad gave me this weird message. It sounded like you'd really found something, and I wanted to see."

Well, I couldn't blame him for that. "Wait here, and I'll show it to you when I get back."

Kevin shifted uncomfortably from one foot to the other. "I thought—I thought maybe I could go with you. Help out or something."

"I no longer require your assistance, any more than you required mine this morning. I work alone." I turned and started toward Brooke's Headquarters.

"Yeah, well, about school today—" Kevin began awkwardly, following me as he spoke.

I heard a sudden noise on the other side of the yard. I put up a hand, cutting Kevin short. Using my keen eyesight—the eye doctor says my vision is better than twenty-twenty—I looked out into the shadows.

A tall, dark form moved toward the Headquarters.

Chapter 7

Tiernay West was tired of sneaking around.

Stealth had its place. Stealth, indeed, was the very thing that had led her to her enemy.

But the dark night wasn't enough to conceal the sound of his footsteps, the sight of his shadowy form. He stood just beyond the entrance to the Mysterious Cult's Headquarters, ready to steal the artifact West sought.

She wouldn't let him have it. She strode boldly forward, ready to meet her foe.

Kevin put a hand on my shoulder as I stepped toward Brooke's Headquarters. "Do you think that's a good idea?" he whispered. He sounded worried—as usual. He might have been an okay guide, but guides have a reputation for bolting at the first sign of trouble.

I ignored him and continued on. Instead of bolting, Kevin followed.

I stopped at the Secret Headquarters' window, and I looked in. As I did, someone opened the door and stepped inside.

Even in the shadows, even though he was dressed all in gray, I knew who it was. Not that I'd ever really doubted it.

"Daryll," I hissed under my breath.

I ducked down beneath the windowsill as Daryll crossed the room.

"Maybe he's looking for the sword for his dad," Kevin whispered.

I rolled my eyes—not that Kevin could tell in the dark. "Why's he sneaking around, then?"

"Why are *we* sneaking around?"

"That's different." I started around the Headquarters, ready to confront Daryll straight on.

"Wait," Kevin said.

I expected him to tell me confronting Daryll was too dangerous, but he whispered, "We could follow him. Find out where he's taking it. And then we can call for help."

"I already told you, I don't need any help." I peered back through the window in time to see Daryll lift a long, narrow object.

"Pay dirt," he said, and started back toward the door.

I almost dashed straight after him. But instead, I crept quietly around the building, watching as he exited the Headquarters.

I would follow the slug to his lair.

Kevin crept around, too, not nearly as quietly. I heard his footsteps in the grass behind me.

Was he planning to follow me all night? Well, I couldn't argue now, not without making even more noise.

Daryll disappeared around Brooke's house. I started after him, Kevin right behind me. I rounded the side of the house just as Daryll stepped into the street. I let him go a block or so, then followed him.

Daryll turned a corner, slipping out of sight. I wanted to chase him, but that would have made noise, too, so I only increased my pace slightly. I heard Kevin's heavy steps on the pavement. Didn't he know anything about stealth?

When I reached the corner, I put up a hand, motioning Kevin to stop, and peered around.

Just in time to see Daryll hop on a bicycle and

ride away. Somehow, he'd tied the sword over the handlebars; the bike wobbled as he rode. He disappeared around another corner.

"Now what?" Kevin whispered. As if he assumed I'd know.

Of course I'd know. The one thing an adventurer is never short on is ideas.

"Every slug leaves a trail," I said. "Now I just need to find Daryll's tracks."

I had experience with bicycle tracks.

I walked down the street, shining my flashlight on the pavement. The rain had stopped, but the street remained damp; I could make out the faint, wet tracks Daryll's tires left on the asphalt.

I followed those tracks, my flashlight making a pool of light in front of me as I walked. Kevin followed.

Daryll was well out of earshot now. "Listen, I'll call when I find the sword. So you can go home now, you know?"

"I know," Kevin said, still following.

Sometimes an adventurer has to be blunt. "I work alone," I snapped. "You're not invited, all right? You're—"

I stopped short, glancing back toward Brooke's house. *I'm starting a club,* she'd said. *You're not invited.*

Kevin's legs were shorter than mine; he panted to keep up. Which meant he made still more noise. I sighed and slowed down again. I needed to walk slowly to keep track of Daryll's bicycle treads, anyway.

A car drove past, catching us briefly in its headlights. Otherwise the night was silent and still. I kept following the tracks. No one was out but me and my prey. Or rather, me and Kevin and my prey.

Either way, Daryll couldn't ride forever. Sooner or later I'd catch up, or else reach the place where he'd taken the sword.

"You know," Kevin said, "I've never been out this late before. It's kind of weird."

"It's *cool.*" I liked the silence, the damp smell of the air, the way the breezes raised goose bumps on my arms.

"Yeah, well, that's what I mean," Kevin said.

Daryll's tracks twisted and turned through the South Newbury streets. A few times, at corners, I slowed down some more to take a closer look at the bicycle treads, figuring out which way he'd turned at intersections. Once, the tracks disappeared into a puddle, and I had to try a couple different directions to figure out where they picked up again. Another time, Daryll rode beneath an awning in front of some shops, and I almost lost him on the dry pavement, but I found his tracks again on the other side.

After a while, the treads stopped turning at corners, and I realized Daryll was heading for the edge of town. Our path took us over a small bridge with a stream trickling beneath it.

"Hey, West?"

I sighed. "Yeah, Kevin?"

"Listen, Tiernay." Kevin stepped around in front of me. "I know I acted really stupid today, okay?" He sounded annoyed—either at himself or at me, I couldn't tell. "After what you did, I should have thanked you or something, not worried about what other people would think."

"Other people are weird," I said. "You learn to ignore them."

"Yeah," Kevin said. "I guess so."

I walked on. So did Kevin. I didn't say he could come, but I didn't try to stop him anymore, either.

Toward the edge of town, at another place where the street met the stream, Daryll's tracks abruptly left the pavement. Deep, muddy tire treads followed the water instead. I turned, following the treads and the stream out of town.

The houses quickly thinned out. A bluff rose to our right, and the few houses I saw on top of it were large and expensive-looking. To the left, across the water, the town gave way to scattered trees, then to forest.

Soon the bluff was taller than me. The stream joined up with the Newbury River, tumbling over rocks and roots. My feet squished in the muddy dirt, no matter how stealthy I tried to be. Somewhere far away an owl hooted. Near the horizon, the clouds broke up and moonlight lit their edges.

Like a true adventurer, I'd left civilization behind.

I turned my flashlight off; the moonlight was just bright enough to see by. Daryll's tracks were deep ruts in the mud now, and I had no trouble following them.

Without warning, those tracks veered away from the river, then ended. A muddy bicycle lay at the foot of the bluff. I looked up. Daryll was nowhere in sight, but his tracks went on, muddy footprints and handprints that led upward. The bluff was now three or four times as tall as me.

"All right!" I said, looking up. "We get to scale the heights."

Chapter 8

The cliff wall was a mile high and sheer as ice. Tiernay West carefully felt for every handhold, every possible foothold, however slight. The going was slow, painfully slow, but though the hours ticked by, she didn't dare rush.

For far below the raging river churned, and any false move would fling her into its icy grasp.

Any wrong step, West knew, would be her last.

"I have acrophobia," Kevin said, looking up.

"What's acrophobia?"

"It means I'm afraid of heights."

"So don't look down."

I set a foot into the face of the bluff. The foot sank into damp earth, making a foothold where there hadn't been one before. I reached up, grabbing a root with one hand, more mud with the other, and I started scrambling up, hand, foot, hand, foot. It was a lot like climbing a tree, only squishier. The moon grew brighter; I could see my own moon shadow on the face of the bluff.

Hand, foot, hand, foot; *squish, squish, squish, squish.* Before I knew it, I was reaching over the edge, pulling myself onto level ground.

My first cliff, successfully scaled. I looked down, proud of my achievement.

Kevin still stood below, looking nervously up.

"Come on," I called.

"I'm trying," Kevin said, though as far as I could tell, all he was doing was staring at the bluff.

The easiest thing would have been to leave Kevin there. I almost did just that, but something made me turn back; I'm not sure what. Maybe it was just that adventurers never do things simply because they're easy.

"Try harder," I said. Kevin didn't move. "I'm sure you can do it," I added, just like Mom did when I was studying for a spelling test.

I didn't expect my words to help, any more than Mom's words had improved my spelling. But Kevin took a deep breath, and he stepped up onto the bluff.

Kevin was a slower climber than me, and he slid

more, too. As he neared the top I reached out and pulled him over the edge. His hands shook, and he was breathing hard. But he hadn't fallen into the river, and I guess that's all that mattered.

While Kevin caught his breath I looked around. The top of the bluff was covered with tall, wet grass. I saw a place where the grass was trampled down—and where Daryll's tracks picked up once more. They led straight to an old house, a few hundred yards away. Even from a distance, even by moonlight, I could tell the house wasn't like the other, more expensive homes around it. The two-story building was smaller, for one thing. Its roof sagged, and in places the walls were broken in. There was no lawn, just the same tall, uneven grass on all sides.

An old, abandoned house. Looked like my sort of place.

I strode forward through the wet grass. Kevin followed, more quickly now that we walked on solid ground.

Water soaked through my jeans. The grass grew taller, wild and deep as an African savanna, and I had to walk slowly to keep from sliding on it. I pulled up a long stem and chewed on one end. The grass tasted like muddy straw; I spat it out again. I wondered whether savanna grass tasted any better.

As I approached the house I saw a porch going all the way around the first floor and a balcony going partway around the second. The paint was peeling; the wood, cracked and splintered. Broken windows were streaked with rain.

I crouched down while we were still at a safe distance, motioning to Kevin to do the same. Together we crept around the house. I tried the side door; it was locked. A few yards away I saw another door, lying flat against the ground: a root cellar, I guessed. As we rounded the front of the house I also saw a road, just a few hundred feet away.

"There was a road?" Kevin squeaked. "We didn't *need* to climb?"

I impatiently motioned him to be quiet. A car was parked on that road, lights off. I dropped flat to the ground; so did Kevin.

I heard the car engine start. Moments later the car drove off. I stood again.

Had Daryll escaped in that car? He was only in middle school, so he wasn't allowed to drive. But then again, he wasn't allowed to steal ancient swords, either.

I turned back to Daryll's tracks. Whether or not he was still here, the sword might be.

Some of his tracks went to the root cellar, but others went to the front door. The ones to the front door looked newer. I followed the trampled grass in that direction.

The porch drooped, uneven gray boards pulling away from one another. I stepped onto the first step slowly, carefully.

The step gave a loud crack; wood gave way beneath my feet. I quickly scrambled up to the next step.

"Hey, what's going on out there?"

A lanky form filled the doorway. I willed my thoughts to be empty and blank, so empty and blank that no one would see me. Just like T. J. Redstone when she was confronted with the leader of the Arakistani assassins—and a king's ransom worth of electronic motion-detection equipment.

A rough hand grabbed my collar. That trick hadn't worked for T. J., either.

Daryll the Slug glared down at me through squinty eyes. I guess he hadn't been in the car after all.

"What are you doing here?" All traces of laziness were gone; Daryll just looked mean. I thought of how he'd once thrown the chopped-up pieces of my first hat at my feet, laughing all the while.

I took a deep breath—not easy when someone is clutching your collar—and looked Daryll straight in the eyes. "I might ask you the same question."

"You might, but I don't have to answer some dumb kid. Now tell me." He shook me by the collar for emphasis. A crude technique.

But an effective one. "I'm looking"—my breath came out in gasps—"for stolen property, of which I believe you have some knowledge."

"You believe wrong, short stuff." Daryll reached out to grip my collar closer. As he did, his hold slackened, just for a moment.

I jerked away from him, and I ran. Daryll chased me through the high, wet grass; it swished as he passed. With his long legs he gained on me fast.

Then all at once the swishing stopped. Startled, I whirled around.

Daryll lay facedown in the grass, barely moving. Kevin stood over him.

"What happened?"

Kevin shrugged. "I tripped him."

"All right!" It felt a little weird, having someone

else disable my enemy. But not half as weird as being strangled by Daryll would have felt. Unlike my classmates, I decided I could appreciate a good rescue.

Daryll moaned, lifted his head to glare at us, and sank back to the grass. He wouldn't stay disabled long.

I headed back for the house. I had a sword to find, after all.

Kevin ran after me. I charged up the stairs, jumping over the step that had cracked before. I flipped on my flashlight and started searching, my heart pounding hard all the while. Kevin kept telling me to hurry up, but he searched, too. We flung open cabinets, shone light into dusty corners, looked for secret doors beneath creaking stairs.

Nothing.

Outside, Daryll yelled, "You're in trouble now!" His footsteps pounded toward the house.

"Time to get out of here," Kevin said.

"Not without the sword!"

"The sword won't do us any good if we're pummeled into dogmeat."

Or fed to the nearest paper cutter. And yet . . . I couldn't leave and give Daryll a chance to move the sword. There had to be something I'd overlooked, some place I hadn't searched.

"The root cellar!" I cried.

Daryll's footsteps grew closer; I heard him crash onto the first step. Then he let out a sharp cry, and I knew the wood had given way beneath his feet, too.

That wouldn't stop him long. I grabbed Kevin's arm and dragged him across the kitchen, through the side door, and out to the root cellar door. The beam of the flashlight wobbled in front of me.

I yanked on the root cellar door. It didn't open. Kevin reached out and slid the rusty metal bolt aside.

It opened. Surprisingly easily for such rusty hinges. As if someone had already been using it. I leaped inside. Kevin yelped as he followed. We fell to the floor several feet below. The flashlight clattered to the ground and went out.

Daryll yelled as he ran after us. I looked up in time to see his shadow fill the doorway.

I expected him to leap into the root cellar after us, and I stumbled to my feet. I didn't intend to give up without a good fight.

Instead, he reached for the cellar door.

"No!" I shouted as I realized what he planned to do. "Get in here and fight like an adventurer!"

Daryll slammed the door shut, leaving us in darkness.

I heard the bolt slide firmly in place.

Chapter 9

The bodies of fallen adventurers littered the tomb.

Some were little more than bones; others reeked with the stench of decaying flesh. A rat peered through the eye socket of a crumbling skull; more rats scurried in the darkness.

Tiernay West allowed herself only a moment to dwell on the fate of those who had come before her. She needed to work fast, or all their deaths would be in vain.

For the dim, dusty tomb was perfectly sealed, and she knew the air inside wouldn't last long.

I slammed my fist against the ceiling, trying to shove the door open, but the bolt held tight.

"Coward!" I yelled, hoping to shame Daryll into coming back and confronting me face-to-face. "You're not worthy of Emma Jensen's memory!"

"Emma Jensen was a fool!" Daryll laughed as he walked away.

Even a slug ought to have more sense of honor than that.

I unclipped the pocketknife from my belt, reaching up to feel for the crack between ceiling and door. I found it, and I tried to use the knife to slide the bolt open, but couldn't seem to get quite the right angle.

"We're trapped, aren't we?" Kevin didn't sound scared, exactly, but he didn't sound not-scared, either. "Did I mention I have claustrophobia?" he asked.

I sighed and turned around. As my eyes adjusted to the dark I saw Kevin pick the flashlight up from the floor. He flipped the switch. The room remained dark. He tapped the lid, shook the flashlight a few times, and flipped the switch again. Light flooded the cellar. Kevin let out a breath, though I would have expected him to be more scared now that he could see just how small the room really was. It was only about ten feet across, and the ceiling was right above our heads. Maybe he didn't really have claustrophobia, but fear of the dark instead. Was there a word for that? Maybe Kevin didn't know it, either.

The floor was made of hard-packed dirt, the walls of large gray stone blocks. The air smelled musty and old. Ancient.

Then my gaze fell on the far corner of the cellar. What I saw there was anything but ancient.

"Wow," Kevin said.

Computers were stacked in that corner. Computers and printers and modems and all sorts of electronics. PROPERTY OF SOUTH NEWBURY ELEMENTARY their labels said.

"You were right, West—there really is treasure here," Kevin said. "I always knew Daryll would grow up to be a criminal, but who knew he'd already started?"

I wasn't waiting to grow up to be an adventurer. Why should I expect my enemies to wait, either?

Kevin began sorting through the equipment. He moved a monitor aside, and behind it I saw—

"Hey, careful!" Kevin yelled as I lunged across the cellar, stumbling over a printer cable.

Behind the monitor lay a sword encased in a battered leather scabbard. I took the sword in my hands, gazing reverently at the sheathed blade. *Treasure*, I thought. *Found and lost and found again.*

The past redeemed. Or one-third redeemed, anyway.

Taking a deep breath, I gripped the sword's hilt, and I pulled it from the scabbard.

It was heavier than I expected; I staggered, then took the hilt firmly in both hands. By the light of the flashlight, the sword didn't look nearly as tarnished as before. Its steel blade shone in the dim cellar. I ran a finger along the blunt side, gingerly touched the sharp side. The sharp side wasn't very sharp. No doubt it had been dulled by years of disuse.

I swung the blade through the air, careful to miss Kevin and all the computer stuff.

"Hey, look out!" Kevin ducked, anyway.

The weight of the sword felt very right in my hands. Like the sort of weapon an adventurer was supposed to wield. I swung it again, savoring my victory. Just then, it didn't seem to matter who my ancestors were.

Kevin went back to sorting through the electronics. "You don't suppose Daryll stole a cell phone, do you? Not that we'd get a signal down here, anyway." He looked up at me abruptly. "How long do you think we have until Daryll comes back?"

"What do you mean?" I'd assumed Daryll was making his way to the border by now, or else booking passage overseas. Yet suddenly I wasn't so sure. The computers and sword were still here, after all. Daryll might be a coward, but he was a greedy coward.

Surely he wouldn't give up on the treasure so easily. Surely he'd come back for it.

I lowered the sword. "He might not actually try to do us in himself," I said, trying to be optimistic. "He might just flood the cellar. Or fill it with fire ants and scorpions." Water would damage the delicate electronics, after all. Fire ants and scorpions would only damage us. "Or he could wait for us to starve. That would work, too."

"You sure know how to make a person feel better, West."

I lowered the sword. I thought of how in Dad's books, finding an artifact was never the end of an adventure; T. J. still had to escape with the artifact and her life both intact. I thought of the mountain guide who said any idiot could get up Mount Everest, but that the tricky part was getting back down again. He was right, too; he died descending Everest the very year he said that.

I didn't intend to follow his example. I swung the sword again, thinking hard. T. J. Redstone says there's always a way out, if you're smart enough and stubborn enough to find it. The sword hit the stone wall. It clanged with a hollow, echoing sound.

Hollow? Echoing? Those weren't normal stone qualities.

I tapped the sword against the rock. This time I knew I hadn't imagined it—I'd heard an echo. I set the sword down and knelt in front of the stone. I found a thin, even seam where the mortar should have been.

I slid the sword into the seam. After only a few inches, it hit empty air. I slid the sword back and forth a few times.

Slowly the stone moved out toward me.

Using both the sword and my hands, I pulled a stone slab out of the wall. It was heavy, much heavier than the sword, but not so heavy I couldn't move it away and set it down on the floor.

I looked at the spot where the stone had been. A tunnel disappeared into the darkness.

"Hey!" Kevin said. "That's our way out of here!" He squinted into the dark. "Or maybe just into more trouble," he said uneasily.

I put the sword back into its scabbard and set it carefully aside. If the tunnel really was our way out, I'd come back around from outside to claim it.

I started into the tunnel on hands and knees, then

looked back at Kevin. His hands were shaking again, and his breathing had sped up. "That's okay," I told him, and realized I meant it. He'd already helped. And not everyone can be an adventurer. Especially not someone with acrophobia, and darkaphobia, and a fear of lemons and ketchup. "I'll come back around for you, too."

But Kevin took a deep breath and said, "I'm going with you, West." He handed me the flashlight.

"Why?"

To my surprise Kevin grinned. "Because I want to know what's in there. Also because I'd rather not face those scorpions alone."

I stared at Kevin, startled. That was the same reason I wanted to go in. Well, the finding-out part, anyway. I was willing to face the scorpions, if I had to.

"Onward!" I said, and leaped—well, crawled—into the tunnel, shining the flashlight ahead of me.

The tunnel was less than half my height; it smelled wet and dusty at once. My hat brushed the damp ceiling as I crawled. Clumps of dirt crumbled around me. The floor was damp, too, soaking through my jeans.

How long since anyone had been in here? Cobwebs brushed my face, leaving sticky, silky strands behind. I heard Kevin panting as he followed me.

The tunnel narrowed, until I was inching along nearly on my stomach. My elbows bumped the walls. My head bumped the ceiling, and dirt fell into my eyes. I wondered whether the tunnel was just going to narrow into a dead end. An adult would have had to turn back by now—the tunnel was too tight—but Kevin and I kept going. Ahead, in the distance, I heard running water.

Without warning, the beam of the flashlight shone on something. Something dark and lumpy.

I stopped abruptly.

"Hey!" Kevin bumped into me.

It was a small bag, half buried in the dirt. The bag might have been velvet once, but the fabric had faded and worn away. I picked it up. There were holes in the velvet; through them I felt something cold and metallic.

My heart began to pound. I wanted to open that bag now, to see if I was right about what was inside. *Three treasures,* I thought. *The second was lost, yet may be recovered.*

Adventurers aren't very good at waiting. But fire

ants and scorpions aren't good at waiting, either. Clutching the bag in one hand and the flashlight in the other, I kept crawling, knowing I'd have time enough to open the bag after we managed our escape.

The tunnel widened out, until it was high enough that I could move on hands and knees again, then higher still. The flashlight lit our way, showing the dirt ahead of us. The darkness seemed to lighten a bit, and then—

I stopped again. Kevin bumped into me again.

"What now?" He didn't sound scared this time, just annoyed.

"Look," I said, shining the flashlight ahead of me. It lit the opening of the tunnel, mere inches ahead. I looked down, over the crumbling edge. The bluff dipped steeply away. Moonlight reflected off the Newbury River, many feet below. If not for the flashlight and the moonlight, we'd have fallen into the churning current—and possibly to our watery deaths.

Kevin drew a sharp breath. "Good call, West. Really, really good call." His voice was low and shaky.

For once, I didn't blame him; I felt a little shaky,

too, on the inside at least. Heights seem a lot higher when you're up above them. Still, I knew we needed to brave those heights once more. Kevin knew it, too; I could tell by the way his breathing sped up. Yet we had to climb, or else languish forgotten in the root cellar. Like that mountain guide had languished on Everest. He'd languished so well I couldn't even remember his name.

Shoving the velvet bag and the flashlight into my pockets, I twisted around and lowered my feet out of the tunnel. I found a firm foothold below me, then gripped the tunnel opening with both hands. It crumbled some more, and I swiftly adjusted my hold.

I'd planned to climb down, but when I looked up, I saw that the top of the bluff was much closer than the bottom. One foothold, one handhold at a time, I made my way first sideways, then upward. After only a few moments I pulled myself over the bluff's edge and onto solid ground.

I leaned over and shone the flashlight down for Kevin. I remembered how much trouble he'd had scaling our last cliff, but before I could offer to go around and unlock the cellar door for him, he reached out and started climbing, carefully, not looking down.

Sooner than I expected, he clambered up beside me, breathing hard but grinning, too. "We did it, West. We really did!"

That still remained to be seen. I handed Kevin the flashlight and pulled the velvet bag from my pocket, telling myself that anything could be inside, lead, or rocks, or somebody's collection of squashed pennies from the zoo. But I didn't believe that. I opened the drawstring bag. Kevin shone the flashlight down as I reached inside.

Dozens of gold coins slid through my fingers.

"Treasure," I whispered.

"Treasure," Kevin agreed, as if he'd never doubted it.

Kevin suggested we follow the road back to town. I agreed, especially once I'd gotten the sword out of the root cellar. I didn't want to lose it to the depths of the Newbury River, any more than I wanted to lose myself there.

On the outskirts of town we came to a pay phone. I stopped, knowing it was time to announce our discovery to the outside world.

I didn't have any money with me. Kevin loaned

me his quarters, which he said he used to play video games.

Reaching the outside world takes a lot of quarters. I waited as the phone rang.

"Hello, Dad?"

"Tiernay?"

"I did it, Dad. I found the treasure! I redeemed the past!" Excitement made my voice squeak. I steadied it. "I'm a real adventurer now!"

"Tiernay, where are you? Is Kevin with you?" Dad didn't sound excited, just worried.

"Gold coins, Dad. Dozens of them. And a sword, too!"

"Tiernay, we've been worried sick about you. I didn't realize it was the middle of the night there until I hung up, or I would have never—" He drew a deep breath. "Your mother, and Greg, and the police have been looking for you. I was about to fly back to the States—"

"Dad."

"I was half-asleep— I didn't realize—"

"Dad!"

"What, Tiernay?"

"It's all right. I'm all right, and Kevin's all right,

too. And we found a bag full of hidden ancient Revolutionary War coins—"

Dad took another deep breath. When he spoke again, his voice was calmer. "That's terrific Tiernay. I'm very proud of you.

"Now I want you to tell me, very slowly and distinctly, exactly where you are."

Chapter 10

Tiernay West stood proudly outside the tomb, another adventure successfully completed. The mystery had been solved, the ancient wrong set right. After braving many perils, West was triumphant once more.

Now she could kick back over a few root beers with her fellow adventurers and recount the dangers she'd faced. Now, she could enjoy a well-earned vacation.

But her vacation wouldn't last long. Already she felt a familiar restlessness.

Soon, West knew, she would venture into the wild once more.

"You're sure this isn't an imposition?" Mom asked Jane Grey, Folklorist, for the third time.

We were in our favorite restaurant, the one Greg had taken us to a few days before. This time, Mom hadn't told me how to dress, even though the restaurant was more brightly lit for lunch than for dinner. I wore jeans, a good T-shirt, comfortable sneakers, and my straw hat. How to dress was one of the few things Mom hadn't told me how to do in the days since she and the police had met us at the pay phone. I'd told Dad that walking home would be easy compared with scaling treacherous cliffs, but he'd insisted I not take another step until Mom and Greg arrived.

Mom firmly held my hand as we stood beside the table.

Already seated, Jane Grey smiled. "The pleasure is entirely mine, I assure you. I look forward to hearing Ms. West's tale directly. I'm sure there are things the newspaper article omitted."

She was right about that. For one thing, the newspaper article got my name wrong. Well, the article titled "Colonial-Era Coins Found in South Newbury" got it wrong. The other article, the police blotter one titled "Lost Children Found," didn't use my name. I'd told Mom that Kevin and I hadn't been lost; we'd known exactly where we were. She didn't seem to find that reassuring.

"All right, then." Mom turned to face me. "I'll be back in an hour. I expect you to still be here. No wandering this time, all right?"

"Of course not." I wasn't on an adventure now, after all.

"Have a nice lunch." Mom turned and went back out to the car.

"Your mother isn't very happy about your adventure, is she?" Jane Grey asked.

"I'm afraid not." The people from the historical society had been excited, and the newspaper reporter. And when I strode into Mr. Jensen's shop, sword in hand (accompanied by a police officer, who needed to include the return in his report), he'd apologized for misjudging me and said I was welcome in his shop any time.

Greg had admitted he was disappointed and hurt that Kevin snuck out without telling him, but mostly he'd said he was just relieved we were okay.

Dad, once he knew I was all right, had listened while I explained all that had happened. He'd told me I was never to use him to get around Mom again; parental permission meant the custodial parent, and that was Mom. But he'd agreed that, otherwise, my adventuring career was off to a fine start.

But Mom had just grounded me. Well, she'd yelled a lot, too, and cried a little, but mostly, she'd told me I couldn't go anywhere for a month. I had tried to explain that I needed to prove myself as an adventurer, to redeem the past and right an ancient wrong, but she hadn't cared. She hadn't even cared that it was her past I'd redeemed. She'd said history was fine and well, but I was in trouble in the present. She'd only let me out for lunch today because I'd already called Jane Grey, and the folklorist had asked her to let me go.

Jane Grey nodded sympathetically. "It's much easier for someone like me. All my children are adults now, and I know that most children manage to grow up just fine. Be patient with your mom, Tiernay. She's worried about you, that's all."

T. J. Redstone's mother had worried about her, too. She'd worried so much that T. J. finally got fed up and cut off all contact, telling her family that she'd moved to Reykjavik (which was sort of true) and they had no phones there (which wasn't true at all).

A waiter—the same waiter as before—came and took our orders. They didn't serve squid or snails for lunch, so I settled on grilled cheese, with a bottle of their best root beer.

The waiter must have remembered me. He served

my root beer in a wineglass, with two cherries and a slice of lime.

"Now, then." Jane Grey's blue eyes brightened; she reached across the table and took my hands in her own. "I want you to tell me everything."

So I did.

I told her about my adventure, and I told her about all the stuff that happened afterward, too.

Like how Daryll really had run for the border, just like I'd expected. Only he'd chosen the wrong border: The police had found him trying to buy a bus ticket to Mexico, even though Canada is a couple thousand miles closer.

Daryll had been arrested, not for stealing the sword, but for stealing the computers from our school. He hadn't worked alone, but with an older kid who had a car—the car we'd seen leaving. The bluff was just a shortcut Daryll took when the car wasn't around.

The other kid had promised to sell the computers to some adult crooks he knew, and to share his ill-gotten gains with Daryll, who apparently no longer found stealing lunch money sufficiently profitable. Only the older kid had gotten mad when Daryll threw in the sword, because ancient swords are harder to sell on the black market than computers.

The police were talking about putting Daryll and the other kid on probation—which is much worse than being grounded—and Daryll had gotten into a lot of trouble with his dad, too.

Katie had also gotten into trouble with Mr. Jensen, but only until she explained that she'd been trying to hide the sword from Daryll, not steal it for herself, because she'd listened in on her brother's phone calls and learned about his plans. Katie knew all about Emma Jensen; her dad had told her and Daryll the story lots of times. She'd read *The Keanes of South Newbury*, too, and had written the words I found on the notebook paper, after hearing them from an aunt of hers.

In spite of Katie's noble intentions, Brooke had kicked her out of the Secret Organization, claiming club members didn't consort with the relatives of criminals like Daryll. Given James Keane, I'd asked Brooke if that meant she couldn't consort with me, either. She'd said it most certainly did. I'd said I was glad, because I don't consort with nonadventurers.

Except Katie's a nonadventurer, and she'd begun sitting with Jessie and me at lunch.

Kevin sat with us, too. He even talked to me at school, though people still laughed at us both. Sometimes he got embarrassed, but sometimes he didn't care. "After you've climbed cliffs and tripped bullies and been trapped in the dark, it's hard to be scared of a few other kids," he'd explained.

Sometimes I wondered whether Kevin had a little bit of adventurer in him, after all.

I also talked to Greg now, which I guess I hadn't done much before. Greg wasn't so bad, once you got to know him. He'd convinced Mom to only ground me for a month, instead of a year. Or the rest of my life, which is what Mom had said she really wanted to do. I still didn't want to see "a lot more" of Greg, but a little more—that might be okay.

The abandoned house belonged to Mr. Jensen; he'd inherited it from a great uncle. Emma Jensen really had once lived there, and the coins really were the Jensen family fortune. Those coins would go to Mr. Jensen once the legal paperwork cleared. He planned to sell some of them to the historical society and keep the rest. He'd also promised Kevin and me a finder's fee. Mom had said my share would be going into my college fund. I hadn't known I had a college fund until then.

"The only thing I haven't figured out," I said at last, "is what the third treasure was." Even though Katie was talking to me again, she wouldn't tell me. She said the answer was too sad.

"Don't you know?" Jane asked. (She'd told me to call her Jane while we were talking; I'd told her to call me Tiernay.) Her voice grew soft. "I think the third treasure must be Emma Jensen."

"Oh." Drowned in the river. *Gone beyond recall.*

That *was* awfully sad—sadder even than when Amelia Earhart disappeared three-quarters of the way around the world. I thought of how Emma Jensen didn't have a flashlight when she went out to hide that gold, and how she went out on a moonless night. It only takes a gust of wind to blow a candle out. Emma Jensen probably never saw the end of the tunnel. She probably fell into the river, just like James Keane said.

Jane raised her coffee mug. "To brave souls everywhere," she said.

I raised my root beer. "To brave adventurers everywhere," I agreed, thinking that Emma Jensen was as brave as they come.

"The amazing thing," Jane said after a moment's respectful silence, "is that there really was buried treasure right in our own backyard. It gives one pause, when old legends turn true. Makes me wonder what else might be hidden right under our noses. Those T. J. Redstone novels might not be so crazy after all."

"You've read Dad's books?"

Jane looked at me, as if not sure what I meant. Then she grinned. "Oh, you're *that* West, are you? That explains a few things. From the perspective of myth and folklore, your father's books are fascinating—not to mention great fun."

"Mom doesn't think so," I said. "Mom still doesn't understand about adventuring at all."

"Oh, I think she understands more than you realize. She's descended from adventurers, after all."

"What do you mean?" I sipped at my root beer. "The Keanes were all traitors and spies. The book said so." At least they probably weren't murderers— but that seemed small consolation.

"There were spies and soldiers on both sides of the war, Tiernay. Your ancestors just happened to be on the losing side. The English weren't as evil for wanting to keep their colonies as school might make it seem. History's more complicated than that."

I nodded. As I did, a movement by the restaurant

door caught my eye. I looked across the room to see Mom walking toward our table. I glanced at my watch. It was 12:58 P.M. in Toronto, which meant an hour really had almost passed.

Mom reached for my hand; I pulled it away. "I'm moving to Reykjavik," I announced.

Mom didn't sigh, but I could tell she was thinking about it.

"I don't suppose," Jane asked, "that I could talk you both into dessert before you book passage overseas?"

"There's no need to go to more trouble on our account," Mom said. Her expression turned strange and a little uncomfortable. As if adventurer talk were a secret club, and she knew she wasn't invited.

Actually, Reykjavik isn't any farther from South Newbury than Los Angeles. I wonder whether T. J. Redstone's mother ever figured that out. I stood, pulled out a chair, and said in my best adventurer voice, "We would be honored if you would join us."

I'd invited Dad to celebrate my first adventure with me, but he'd said he had some research to finish in Vladivostok first. Yet Mom laughed a little—the first time she'd laughed since I found the treasures—and said in her best Mom voice, "I would be honored, too."

Jane ordered crème brûlée, because, like Dad and T. J., she speaks French. Mom and I ordered in English, because that's the language in which chocolate cheesecake is written. As I savored my dessert I thought about how T. J. Redstone had traveled to Arakistan, to Juaraja, to the Keroon. One day I would visit places like that, too. I would visit places that didn't even have names yet. Maybe not right away—first I had to get ungrounded, then finish elementary school—but it's never too soon for an adventurer to start preparing.

For I was no longer an adventurer-in-training. I was Tiernay West, Professional Adventurer. And already I was eager to get back out and explore. I'd start with South Newbury, because like Jane said, old legends had turned true here. Also because you have to start somewhere, en route to the far reaches of the earth.

"From now on," I announced, "the only way I plan to redeem history is by making more of it."

Mom laughed again. I wondered whether one day she really would understand better about adventuring, if I was patient like Jane Grey said. Adventurers aren't good at being patient—but if T. J. Redstone could wait six months to translate a single coded missive, if Dad could wait five years for the first T. J. book to sell—maybe I could wait, too.

Jane smiled at me over a spoonful of crème brûlée, the serious smile of a fellow adventurer who already understands completely.

"Tiernay West," she said, "I don't doubt that in the least."